Secrets

OF

Willow Springs

BOOK 3

The Amish of Lawrence County Series

Tracy Fredrychowski

ISBN 978-1-7342411-7-4 (paperback)
ISBN 978-1-7342411-6-7 (digital)

Copyright © 2021 by Tracy Fredrychowski
Cover Design by Tracy Lynn Virtual, LLC
Cover Photograph by Jim Fisher

All Bible verses are taken from New Life Version Bible (NLV) and the New King James Version (NKJV)

Published in South Carolina by The Tracer Group, LLC-
https://tracyfredrychowski.com

Contents

A Note about Amish Vocabulary

The language the Amish speak is called Pennsylvania Dutch and is usually spoken rather than written. The spelling of commonly used words varies from community to community throughout the United States and Canada. Even as I researched this book, some words' spelling changed within the same Amish community that inspired this story. In one case, spellings were debated between family members. Some of the words may have slightly different spellings. Still, all come from the interactions I have with the Amish settlement near where I was raised in northwestern Pennsylvania.

While this book was modeled upon a small community in Lawrence County, this is a work of fiction. The names and characters are products of my imagination and do not resemble any person, living or dead, or actual events in that community.

List of Characters

Daniel Miller. The twenty-one-year-old English brother to Emma Byler.

Katie Yoder. Samuel's younger *schwester* and Emma's best friend.

Emma Byler. (aka Elizabeth Cooper) Sixteen-year-old Amish sister to Daniel.

Samuel Yoder. Emma's special friend and *bruder* to Katie

Bishop Shetler. Church leader in Sugarcreek and *doddi* to Daniel and Emma.

Jacob Byler. Emma's Amish *datt.*

Rebecca & Anna Byler. Emma's older twin *schwesters*.

Matthew Byler. Emma's older Amish *bruder.*

Sarah Mast. Matthew's special friend.

Marie Cooper. Biological mother to Daniel and Emma.

Nathan Bouteright. Marie's husband.

Levi and Ruth Yoder. Katie and Samuel's parents.

Map of Willow Springs

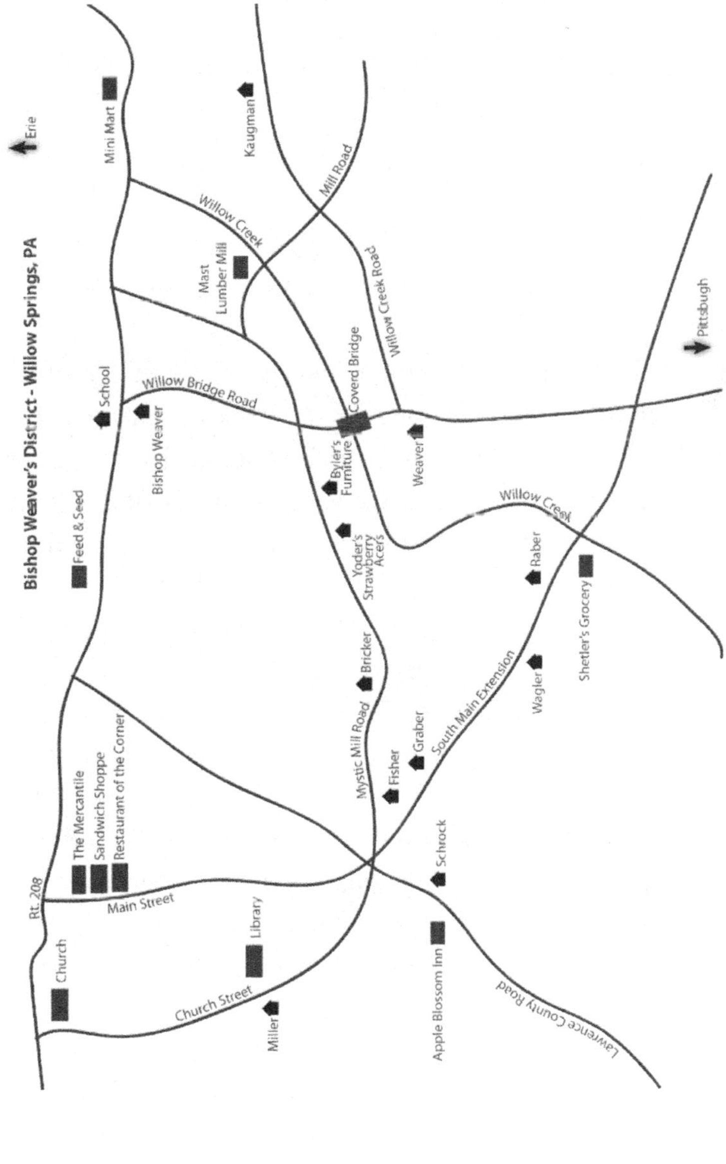
Bishop Weaver's District - Willow Springs, PA
Erie
Mini Mart
Kaugman
Mill Road
Willow Creek
Mast Lumber Mill
Willow Creek Road
Pittsburgh
School
Willow Bridge Road
Bishop Weaver
Coverd Bridge
Byler's Furniture
Weaver
Feed & Seed
Willow Creek
Yoder's Strawberry Acers
Raber
Shetler's Grocery
Bricker
Wagler
South Main Extension
Mystic Mill Road
Graber
Fisher
The Mercantile
Sandwich Shoppe
Restaurant of the Corner
Schrock
Rt. 208
Main Street
Library
Church
Apple Blossom Inn
Church Street
Miller
Lawrence County Road

Prologue

December 31, 2017 - Willow Springs, PA

Daniel Miller stood behind his sister, Emma, protecting her from the ice pellets stinging the back of his neck. He waited for her to tell him she was ready to leave. Everyone who came to pay their last respects had already added a shovel of dirt to the top of her mother's grave and went to their waiting buggies. She didn't make a sound, frozen to the spot she had claimed as her own for the past hour, ignoring his pleas to go back to the house and out of the cold.

The sound of metal wheels on the frozen ground disappeared, replaced by an unnerving quiet. The last of the buggies pulled away from the Amish Cemetery, leaving his truck alone amidst the small white grave markers. He pressed the remote starter in his pocket before trying to convince her again to leave. Frozen rain gathered on Emma's black wool coat as he rubbed his hands on her upper arms and rested his chin on top of her thick brown bonnet.

"The temperature is dropping. Will you please let me take you home now?"

A sob lodged in Emma's throat. It took Daniel a few seconds to understand what she was trying to say. "I don't want to leave," her voice labored.

He pulled her close. "I know, but she wouldn't want you standing out here in the cold either."

"I can't believe she's gone. This was *Gott's* will, but how am I ever going to live without her?"

He turned her around and guided her to his truck. "For a while, I'm sure it will be hard."

No sooner had they made it to the truck when a van pulled up beside them. Barely waiting for the white vehicle to come to a complete stop, the side door slid open, and Nathan Bouteright and their English mother, Marie Cooper got out.

"Mom, Nathan, you came. How did you get permission to leave Ohio?" Daniel asked.

Nathan reached out to shake Daniel's hand. "It took some doing, but we finally got her probation officer to sign the release allowing her to travel to Pennsylvania. We would have been here sooner, but Interstate 80 was a sheet of ice. Our driver couldn't go any faster than forty miles an hour."

It didn't take Emma any time at all to find her way to Marie's open arms.

"Oh, Momma, it happened so fast. The doctors hoped the chemo would help, but cancer had already spread to her bones."

Marie wrapped both arms around the girl and pulled her close. "I'm sorry I couldn't make it here faster."

Daniel blew warm breath into his cupped hands. "Maybe you'll have better luck getting her out of the cold. I'm having a hard time getting her to leave."

Marie broke the embrace long enough to look in her daughter's eyes. "Emma, it's freezing out here. You're not going to do anyone any good if you end up sick. Please, the van is warm."

Emma let her mother guide her to the open door, nodding her head in agreement.

"Have your driver follow me," Daniel instructed.

~~

Emma took comfort in the warm vehicle making her way to the bench seat in the back. Marie took a seat in the second row and moved over so Nathan could sit beside her. It didn't take but a few minutes to catch up to the procession of yellow-topped buggies making their way back to the Byler farm. The stillness in the van lingered by the slow journey through the back roads of Willow Springs. An overwhelming sadness filled Emma at the thought of returning to the comforts of her *mamm's* kitchen without her in it.

The announcer on the radio reminded her that it was the last day of two thousand and seventeen. A year that would be etched in her memory for the rest of her life. The cold glass eased the pounding in her head as she rested against the window. She closed her eyes and tried to remember her *mamm's* smile as she thought. *Will I always remember her face so vividly? Or the way she smelled of spring lilacs and what her voice sounded like when she called my name?*

Fresh tears spilled down her cheeks when she opened her eyes, seeing Nathan whisper something in her mother's ear. Three months had passed since leaving Sugarcreek to come home to help care for her ailing *mamm*, but by the looks of things, Marie had found her own contentment with Nathan. A deep emptiness filled her, but for a quick second, at least, it was replaced with a genuine gladness for her English mother's happiness.

The window fogged over, and she wiped a small opening as she realized they were about to pass Yoder's Strawberry Acres. Within a few minutes, they would pull into her *datt's* driveway, and she'd have to face hundreds of neighbors waiting to pay their condolences. She was sure they meant well, but all she wanted to do was retreat to the privacy of her room. The next few hours would be harder on her than the last six months. Only her closest friends, Samuel and Katie Yoder, and her immediate family, knew she wasn't really Emma Byler. However, she was Emma Byler through and through, even if her birth certificate stated she was Elizabeth Cooper.

Not wanting to leave the warmth of the van, Emma stayed still as the driver took direction from Nathan. The porch outside her window reminded her of one of the last good days her *mamm* had. They sat in the white rockers enjoying a late warm spell, drinking a glass of her favorite mint tea. It was her *mamm* who had reminded her to stop trying to write her story. She told her only *Gott* knew the next chapter. Her job was to have enough faith to trust Him, whatever that might be. At the time, little did she know the next chapter would be this.

~~

After pulling up beside the van, Daniel walked to the side and opened the door. Nathan stepped out and turned to hold his hand to help Marie from her seat, and Daniel smiled at the gentleness in which Nathan treated his mother. While he decided to stay in Willow Springs when he brought Emma home, he didn't witness how close they had become over the last few months. Even with the bleakness of the day, he winked when he caught his mother's eye.

Marie looked toward Emma. "Are you ready?"

Emma crawled around the middle seat and pulled her bonnet tight to ward off the wind that swept into the van.

Nathan guided the girls up the stairs, and Daniel stopped when he saw Bishop Shetler standing near the front door. He reached up and pulled Marie's coat to get her attention. "What's he doing here?"

"Hush!" Marie said, spinning her head back. "He's Emma's grandfather as well, and I assume he's here for the same reason everyone else is. Please don't make a scene. Be cordial for Emma's sake, at least."

Nathan walked up the stairs and stopped to shake the bishop's hand before holding the door open for Emma and Marie. Without saying a word or making eye contact, Daniel took the door from Nathan and let him follow his mother and sister into the house.

A stern voice rang behind him. "Daniel, can I have a word with you?"

"I think the time for a word or two is long past," Daniel said, not missing a beat. "I don't have anything to say to you." As quickly as he opened the door, he let it close, leaving his grandfather out in the cold.

Chapter 1

Mixed Emotions

Pressure started to build in Daniel's chest and a throbbing ache settled behind his eyes with distaste for his Amish grandfather. From across the room, Bishop Shetler moved around, shaking hands and speaking as if he had every right in the world to be there. With every glance, he blamed him for the abuse he endured as a child. The agony of realizing he had family all along haunted him. Their lives would have turned out so different if only the bishop had claimed him when he had the chance. Let alone sending Emma off to be raised by Jacob and Stella Byler. Emma's life surely would be different if Melvin didn't play God with their lives.

The way he saw it, his biological father knew all along Melvin couldn't be trusted to do the right thing. Perhaps, that is why his father left his Amish family behind and chose the English world instead. If this is the way his family faced challenges, he was better off being English.

His hand felt clammy against his bouncing knee as his grandfather talked to his mother in hushed tones, he tried to ignore their huddled stance. Nothing good would come of knowing his family's true identity, however, discovering Emma was his biological sister was a small light in an otherwise dismal situation.

From where he sat in the corner of the room he focused on Emma and let out a slow breath when her older sisters, Rebecca and Anna, pulled her from the stairs and into the kitchen. His pulse quickened as the room seemed to close in around him. With Emma with her sisters, he stood to leave.

~~

Rebecca grabbed Emma's arm and muttered. "If we have to stay downstairs, so do you."

Emma pleaded. "I want to go lie down for a few minutes. I promise I won't be gone long."

Anna sat at the table and leaned on her elbow. "We all want to escape to our rooms, but it wouldn't be fair if we left *Datt* to tend to all of these people himself."

Rebecca's jaw quivered. "If anyone deserves some alone time, it's Anna and me."

"How do you figure that?" Emma asked in a defensive tone.

Anna interrupted. "Rebecca, don't go there. This is not the time or place."

Emma didn't back down from Rebecca's comment and asked. "Again, why do you think you and Anna warrant any more time than I do?"

Rebecca held her hand up to stop Anna from adding anything and turned back to Emma. "You weren't even here for most of *Mamm's* illness. We held this family together while you were off with your English mother. Now you want to come back and act as if your grief is as deep as ours."

The shock of her *schwester's* words stung, and unyielding tears spilled over on her cheeks. She dropped her head and looked over to Anna, hoping for compassion in her other *schwester's* eyes.

Anna shook her head. "Rebecca, that was uncalled for. You know as well as I do, she's as much a part of this family as we are. No matter what a piece of paper says."

Rebecca waved them both off and turned to leave. "I'm laying it out there as I see it."

In the chair beside Anna, Emma crossed her arms on the table and buried her head.

Anna rubbed a small circle in the center of Emma's back and bent in close. "Please don't pay her any attention; you know how she gets. Tomorrow she won't even remember she said such hurtful words. She's lashing out. Who better to do that to than her *schwesters.*"

Emma turned her head toward Anna but kept her cheek pressed against her doubled arms. "I suppose so."

Anna stood, pushed the wrinkles out of her apron, and looked toward the living room. "I'm not even sure who some of these people are. Who is that man talking to your mother?"

Emma looked past Anna. "Bishop Melvin Shetler, my *doddi*, and the woman sitting in the chair next to him is Lillian, my *mommi*."

"Your grandparents?"

"*Jah.* A shocker, right? I go to meet my mother and find out I have grandparents, as well."

"We've been so busy I failed to ask you about your summer in Sugarcreek."

She patted Anna on the arm. "Don't think twice about it. The whole story is so twisted I can't even keep it straight." Taking her *schwester* by the arm, she said, "Come, *Mamm* would want us to make sure everyone is comfortable. Besides, I wouldn't want to give Rebecca any more fuel for her fire."

~~

Marie looked toward the door as Daniel left and said, "Give him some time. He'll come around. He's hurting right now, and you're receiving the brunt of his frustration."

Melvin glanced over his shoulder toward the door and the spitting image of his deceased son Jake flashed before his eyes. "What concerns me the most is he's so much like Jake, and we all know how well I handled that situation. I'm older now, and I hope I can prevent history from repeating itself."

Nathan rested his hand in the small of Marie's back and bowed into their conversation. "I've spent time with the boy. He's got a good head on his shoulders. I can't imagine he'll become anything like the stories Marie tells me of your son. What Jake found so exciting about the English world; Daniel's already experienced for the last twenty-one years."

Bishop Shetler pulled on his long white beard. "It's not the influences in his life that worry me. It's the hatred in his eyes. I saw the same thing in Jake the day I told him he was being put under the *bann* for drinking."

Nathan looked toward Marie and then back at Melvin before saying. "Again, Daniel isn't Amish, so I think you may be reading more into the situation than you need to. Give him time; he'll come around."

"Let's hope so," Melvin stated.

~~

Regardless of how he wanted to be there for Emma, Daniel couldn't stay a minute longer and watch his grandfather. How dare he show up and act as if he had a right to be a part of Emma's life? He gave up that right sixteen years ago when he turned his back on his grandchildren like they were nothing more than a blemish to his precious pride.

4

Taking the steps two at a time, he picked up his pace as he moved toward his truck. When he reached the door, he heard his name and turned toward his best friend Matthew Byler's familiar voice.

"Daniel, wait."

Matthew left the barn and walked toward his ice-covered vehicle, pulling his collar up to shield the wind from his face.

"I was coming back into the house for you. It was so crowded in there I decided to hold out in the barn for a while." Matthew motioned his head in the direction of the wooden structure. "I started a fire in the wood stove in the tack room."

Daniel fell in step with Matthew, tucking his keys back in his pocket as they walked. "Sorry about your mother."

Matthew adjusted his black wool hat to shield the ice pellets swirling in front of the double doors. "It was *Gott's* will to take her, and not my job to question Him."

Confused by his friend's unemotional response, he asked. "She was so young. Don't you question why God would take her from you and your sisters so early?

Matthew waited a few minutes as he opened the tack room door and sat on a stool close to the fire. A small block of wood and pocketknife sat on the workbench, and he resumed working with them while he responded. "This is the end to her earthly life, but *Gott* willing, her life continues."

Daniel straddled the stool next to him. When it was evident Matthew said all he was going to say about his mother, he changed the subject.

"Have you given any more thought to Nathan's offer to board horses here in Willow Springs?"

"I need to talk it over with my *Datt*. I'm expecting things will calm down some, and I can tell him my plans. I've started fixing fences and making new stalls in case it works out."

5

He laid down the knife and picked up a piece of sandpaper. "I saw Nathan and your mother made it today. I'm sure Emma appreciates them being here."

The window that overlooked the house was starting to ice over and Daniel rubbed a small spot to clear his view. "Emma's amazing. After all she's been through, I thought she might carry a chip on her shoulder as big as a boulder."

Matthew looked up at his friend and asked, "By the look of how you glare at Bishop Shetler, maybe it's you with a chip on your shoulder. Anything you want to talk about?"

"Nothing a cold beer and a good time won't cure."

"Not so sure about that, but you know where I am if you need a friend."

Daniel slapped Matthew on the back. "Do you want to join me?"

Matthew shook his head from side to side. "Are you sure that's the way you want to solve the problems with your grandfather? I'd say drinking will only make things worse."

Daniel dug his keys out of his pocket and stood to leave. "Tell Emma I'll be back in a few days to check on her, and in the meantime, I'm sure you'll take care of our sister just fine."

Daniel pulled his collar up the moment he stepped outside. A row of yellow-topped buggies added color to an otherwise gloomy day. He couldn't get over the disappointment on his mother's face when he protested his grandfather's presence. If she thought for one minute he'd welcome him into his life with open arms, she had another thing coming, and where did Matthew get off judging him for wanting a drink? He knew of more than one Amish man who resorted to tipping a bottle to get through the day. The problem was they hid it away so their precious image wouldn't be tarnished. Like his grandfather, it was more important to put on a show than face the truth out in the open.

The truck door handle, encased in ice, matched his heart at that moment. Matthew would never understand what he went through. More importantly, how could he ever forgive the one man who left him there to face the evil in the world alone.

Under his breath, he mumbled when the engine rumbled. "I don't need any of you!" He hit the gas a bit too hard, swerving on a patch of ice as he left.

~~

The screech of tires turned everyone's head toward the window as a puff of smoke left an unsettling silence in the air. Emma looked toward her mother and saw her drop her head as Nathan whispered something in her ear. She sensed her mother's displeasure across the room but was grateful Nathan was there to comfort her. She certainly understood Daniel's reaction to Bishop Shetler. Still, she had not seen this side of her brother, and it concerned her.

The warmth of her best friend Katie Yoder's hand on her shoulder pulled her attention back to their conversation.

"What do you think?" Katie asked.

"I'm sorry. What do I think about what?"

"Getting together in a few days to work on ideas for the bakery. It might not be what you want to think about right now, but it would take your mind off things for a few hours."

Emma watched as her *datt* walked around the room, making sure he spoke to each person individually. Even though she heard what Katie was asking, she couldn't help but watch the exchange between her grandfather and her *datt*. Their familiarity with each other bothered her, and it only reminded her of the secrets they shared. She was glad she learned the truth about her birth parents and even enjoyed a friendly relationship with Marie, but she understood how Daniel felt. There was something about the way the bishop pushed his responsibility aside that bothered her. For now, she would be cordial and show the utmost respect for her *doddi*, but she had questions as well.

Turning her attention back to Katie, she said, "I think I'd like that. *Mamm* was excited about our plans, and she'd want us to keep the ball moving."

Katie reached out to touch Emma's arm. "Do you want to come to my house, or do you want to get together here?"

"I think it would do me good to get out. I'll come to your *haus*."

Katie looked in the front room for her parents. "I'll ask *Mamm* what day might be best. She took over the bread order for the Sandwich Shoppe and she'll need my help filling the orders."

Emma sighed. "I forgot about that. When did she take over my *mamm's* order?"

"Right after you left for Sugarcreek, I think?"

Rebecca returned to the kitchen and plopped down beside Emma on the bench. Emma turned toward her *schwester* and asked. "Was *Mamm* feeling poorly before I left for Sugarcreek?"

With a snip in her voice, Rebecca said, "You were so wrapped up in yourself, you didn't even notice. We thought it was because you left, but when she didn't start feeling better, *Datt* made her go to the doctor. I wanted to write to you and tell you to come home and help, but she made us swear to leave you be."

The tissue in Emma's hand tore in two when she realized she missed so many months with her mother. She should have stayed in Willow Springs, where she belonged, and it was apparent Rebecca was angry with her for going. It might take some doing for Rebecca to forgive her, but could she forgive herself?

Katie reached for her hand and said, "There was nothing you could do even if you did stay home. Your *mamm* knew you needed to be with your birth mother, and she wouldn't want it any other way."

Katie tilted her head toward Rebecca. "Shame on you for making her feel bad for not being here."

Rebecca responded curtly. "What do you know? You didn't watch her cry at missing her precious Emma. She acted like Anna and I weren't around, even though we cared for her and kept this house running smoothly."

She hissed toward Emma. "All she wanted was you. How do you think that made Anna and I feel?"

The anger in Rebecca's eyes pierced a piece of Emma's heart at the strain she'd put on her family. "I had no idea. Why didn't you tell me sooner?"

Rebecca stood to leave. "*Mamm* asked us not to, and Anna is too nice to stir up trouble."

Rebecca left the room, and Katie slid closer to Emma on the bench and rubbed the back of Emma's hand. "Now, don't you pay no never mind to her. She's angry, and it's easier to blame you than to face the fact she's grieving. We both know how she deals with things. She gets mad, says hurtful things, and moves on. I bet before the day is over, she'll come and apologize."

Emma wiped a tear from the corner of her eye with the back of her hand. "I highly doubt it. She holds a grudge for a long time, and if she's this upset with me, I can count on it lasting a long while. My only hope is Anna can talk some sense into her, and she'll calm down.

Chapter 2
Hiding Daniel

Day turned into night, and the last of the buggies pulled away from the Byler farm, and Emma could escape to the privacy of her room. Marie and Nathan had stayed the night and already went to bed in two rooms across the hall. The look on her English mother's face when she looked at Nathan, made her smile on such a heart wrenching day. He was a great influence, and in no time the community in Sugarcreek would accept Marie.

Emma removed her *kapp* and unpinned her hair. A soft knock on the door drew her attention to her late-night visitor.

"Emma, are you still awake?"

The door opened, and Emma waved Marie in. Her mother quietly closed the door and Emma pointed to the hope chest at the end of the bed. She turned to Marie and ran the wooden hairbrush through her waist-length wheat-colored hair.

Marie held her hand out, "May I?"

Emma turned her back to her and flipped her hair over her shoulder as Marie guided the brush through the long locks.

In a whisper, Marie said, "Thank you."

"For what?"

"For this. For letting me be a part of your life."

Emma looked over her shoulder and saw the tenderness in Marie's eyes and couldn't help but be moved by the emotion. "I'm sure today was hard for you."

10

"I was nervous coming. I wasn't sure how your dad would react to me being here, but he's been gracious, and I'm grateful for that. Having Nathan by my side certainly helped ease my anxiety."

Emma smiled when she saw the twinkle in her mother's eyes when she spoke Nathan's name. "So, things are going well between the two of you?"

Color rose to Marie's cheeks. "Better than well. I'm still living in the *doddi* house and taking care of the children during the day. Of course, Rosie makes sure we're never alone, per the bishop's request. Nathan's been wonderful, and he's been encouraging me to meet with the bishop, and he and the children are trying to teach me to speak the language. Thank goodness my mother was Mennonite, so I have some knowledge of Pennsylvania Dutch, but I still have a lot to learn."

"Are you going to join the church?"

"Nathan is hoping I will."

"What do you want?"

Marie took a few minutes to gather her thoughts and removed a tangle from Emma's hair before she answered. "I want to feel like I belong. I want a family, and I'm beginning to think Nathan can give me those things."

Emma reached up to take her hand in her own. "I'm so happy for you."

Marie swallowed hard before saying. "You have no idea how happy you've made me. I'll never replace Stella and the lifetime of memories you have with your Amish mother, but I am ever so thankful that God gave us another chance."

Emma turned on the bed toward her mother. "Do you think *Gott* put me back in your life because he knew *Mamm* was going to die?"

Tears balanced on Marie's eyelashes as she pulled Emma into a tender hug.

"I'm sure of it. He knows all things, and I believe He answers prayers when we need them the most."

~~

A new day began with plenty of sunshine and a warm embrace. Marie and Nathan said their goodbyes and left for Sugarcreek. With a promise to visit in the spring, Emma waved from the porch and went back inside.

Once inside, she leaned back on the blue door and thanked *Gott* for bringing Marie into her life. Her *datt* sat in his rocker across the room with his head tipped back and his eyes closed. Emma quietly made her way to his chair, sat on the floor, and laid her head in his lap. Without saying a word, he placed his hand on top of her head.

"Thank you for coming home when you did. It meant the world to your *mamm,* and you made her last few months peaceful."

Without lifting her head, Emma said. "The house will be so quiet without her."

"That it will. I'm sure it will take all of us some time to get used to her not being with us."

Listening to him speak of her with a crack in his voice made Emma draw in a sob. They sat still for a few minutes before she heard her father take in a deep breath and ask, "Will you be staying home for a while?"

Alarmed by his question, she lifted her head. "Where else would I go? This is my home, and it always will be."

"I see how you are with Marie. I assumed you'd want to move to Sugarcreek to be close to her."

"*Datt*, we haven't seen eye to eye on many things this year, but please understand, this is my home. You are my *datt*. Anna and Rebecca are my *schwesters,* and Matthew is my *bruder*. Yes, Marie is my mother, and Daniel is my brother, but Willow Springs is and will always be my home, I hope."

Emma covered his calloused hand with her own. "I have no desire to live anywhere else, and as long as I'm welcome here, I hope to stay forever."

With his eyes misting over, the gray hairs in his beard, and the lines around his eyes looked deeper. The last year had aged him, and for a few moments, as she looked at the man who always held her up, she realized he needed her as much as she needed him. She squeezed his fingers; his chest rose as he labored to keep his emotions under control. There were no words that either of them could speak to ease the pain. Instead of trying to reason with it, Emma laid her head back in his lap and closed her eyes.

~~

Throughout the next day, food continued to show up and it took no effort to warm supper up from the array of choices in the crowded refrigerator. At the start of the meal, a knock at the front door forced Matthew up from his spot.

"Daniel, you're in time. The girls just put supper on the table. Would you like to join us?"

Without answering, Daniel reached for the door frame to steady his wavering body.

Looking back over his shoulder, Matthew hollered. "It's Daniel, don't wait for me; go ahead and eat. I'll grab something later."

He pulled the door shut, wrapped his arm around his staggering friend, and led him off the porch toward the barn.

"Confound it, Daniel, what are you doing showing up like this?"

"I ...I... thought my best buddy woo...uld hang out with meeee."

13

"We'll hang out alright, right here until you sleep this off or sober up, whichever comes first."

"Ahhh, buddyyyy. Don't be a partyyyy pooper." He slurred, jabbing a finger into Matthew's chest.

Matthew struggled to open the hefty door while holding Daniel up. "Where's your truck?"

Daniel waved his hand. "Wrapped around the signnn."

Matthew pushed Daniel through the door onto a bale of hay. "Don't move; I'll be right back."

"Okay, buddddy," Daniel slurred before rolling to the floor.

~~

Anxious to talk to Daniel, Emma hurried through supper and carried her plate to the sink before reaching for her coat and scarf off the peg by the back door. She stopped beside Anna and uttered. "It's my turn to wash dishes, but do you mind helping Rebecca?"

Rebecca pushed her chair away from the table in a huff. "There you go again, pushing your chores off on us to do who knows what!"

Rebecca's sharp tone lingered in the air as Emma looked toward her *datt,* waiting for his response to Rebecca's outburst.

Without looking up from his paper, Jacob harshly replied, "Rebecca, that will be about enough from you. I warned you once about your place in this family. Do I need to do so again?"

Emma hoped he'd give her permission to continue outside. When her *datt* motioned her to the sink, she hung her coat and scarf back on the peg.

"Your visit can wait until the kitchen is readied back up," he barked.

"Yes, sir," was all she said as they all worked in unison without saying a word.

Emma picked up a towel and waited for Rebecca to fill the sink. Rebecca clanked the dishes in the drainer, smirking that Emma didn't get her way. Anna, who was always known for her peacemaking abilities, lightened the mood by asking a series of questions.

"Emma, tell us about the plans you and Katie have for the bakery. We sure could use something fun to talk about for a few minutes."

Rebecca pulled in a deep breath and blew it out as loudly and obnoxiously as possible. "See what I mean, it's always about Emma and what Emma's doing. There's more to this family than Emma, Emma, Emma!"

Jacob slapped the table and stood, towering over his daughters. "Rebecca, go to your room."

"I'm nineteen, don't you think I'm a little old to be sent to my room?"

"As long as you're in my *haus,* you'll do as I say, and if you act like a child, you'll be treated like one." With one swipe of his hand, he pointed toward the steps. "Go!"

Rebecca snatched the towel from Emma's grasp, dried her hands, and threw it back.

Jacob's words echoed off the bare white walls as Rebecca took the stairs two at a time.

"I assume you won't show your face again until you go to *Gott* about whatever's eating you."

Both Anna and Emma stood still as their *datt* gathered his hat and headed to the door. "I have a few orders to work on." The door rattled behind him.

Anna let out a slow and steady "Whew..."

Emma sunk her hands in the soapy water and asked, "Do you know why she's so upset with me?"

"I do."

"Please tell me. I can't fix it if I don't know what it is."

Anna took a plate from Emma's hand. "I don't think you can. I tried to talk to her, but she can't see past *Mamm* being so heartsick while you were away. She feels like she hung the moon on you, and we were nothing but falling stars."

Emma continued to wash the stack of plates and asked, "Do you feel the same?

"Rebecca and I may be twins, but our compassion level is completely different. I understand why you had to leave. And if you knew how sick *Mamm* was, you would have come home…I'm sure of it."

With a longing in her voice, Emma answered, "If only I'd known."

Anna stopped, looked toward the steps, and leaned in closer. "She also thinks *Mamm* might have held on longer if she wasn't so upset. And on top of that, she's jealous of you."

"Of me? But why?"

"You got to leave this farm and explore Sugarcreek. You could jump the fence, and nobody would say a word. But most of all, you still have a mother."

Emma sank in a chair at the table and rested her chin in her hands. "I had no idea she felt that way."

Anna patted her shoulder. "You had no control over any of this. Rebecca doesn't see that yet. Give her some time; she'll come around."

"Oh Anna, what am I going to do about all of this?"

"I'm not sure. Go to *Gott* and let Him figure it out. We both learned from *Mamm* we have no control in writing our story. *Gott* knew we would be right here, right now, facing these challenges. I believe things happen for a reason, and He must have something special planned for our lives along the way. Why else would he take her, other than to teach us something we can use later in life?"

"You think so? How can Rebecca be so mad at something orchestrated by *Gott*?"

16

Anna dried the last few dishes and placed them in the cupboard before answering. "I suspect Rebecca being mad at you has nothing to do with you, but more with *Gott* trying to show her something."

"I suppose so. But I don't like it either way."

"Again, it's not our place to question *Gott* on anything He does or doesn't do. Our job is to put our faith in Him and let Him take care of the rest."

Emma tucked a loose strand of hair back under her *kapp* and asked, "How did you get so smart?"

"I don't think I'm smart. I'm just a good listener and put my trust in *Gott*. The kitchen is tidy now, why don't you go visit with Daniel."

"I think I will."

She pulled Anna in for a quick hug. "Thank you for always being so sweet."

~~

The night air took Emma's breath away as she tied a blue scarf over her *kapp* and walked to the barn. The glow in the tack room window guided her way as she faced the double doors, opening them only wide enough to slip through. Light filtered on the floor, cascading a shadow on Daniel, she dropped to her knees and rolled him over. Laying her hand across his forehead, she thanked *Gott* when he felt warm.

"Matthew, where are you?"

When he didn't answer, she hollered louder. "Matthew!"

The rumble of tires on the frozen ground averted her attention to the door. Not wanting to leave, she tilted in closer. "Daniel, are you okay? Please wake up." When he didn't respond, she reached for the horse blanket thrown over the stall door and covered him before heading outside to look for Matthew. She reached the door but Matthew pushed her back inside and shut it behind them.

"You shouldn't be out here. Go back inside where it's warm."

"I wanted to visit with Daniel, but I think he's hurt."

"Oh, he's hurt alright, but a self-inflicted pain he'll suffer more from tomorrow."

Confused by his cold-hearted pitch, she raised her eyebrows and looked his way.

Matthew sat on the bale of hay. "He's not hurt; he's drunk."

"Drunk?"

"Can't you smell him? He wreaks of stale beer."

"I didn't think he drank."

"Me neither, but I guess there's lots of things we don't know about him."

"Should we take him in the *haus*? He'll freeze to death out here."

"That's the last thing we need to do. *Datt* still isn't so sure about him. Taking him inside will only cause trouble. You go back inside, and I'll stay out here and keep the fire going in the wood stove until he sleeps it off."

"*Datt* is out in the shop working. What if he catches him like this?"

"He won't, as long as Daniel is here, he won't come into the barn. When he goes to bed, I'll fix the sign."

"What's wrong with it?"

"Looks like Daniel missed the driveway and ran right into it. I'm trusting I can fix it before *Datt's* any wiser."

"We shouldn't keep that from him, should we?"

"Probably not, but *Gott* willing he won't discover it, and Daniel will be long gone before morning."

"I'm worried. This isn't like Daniel."

Matthew took his hat off and balanced it on his knee. "I'm not sure what happened in Sugarcreek, but something set him off. Do you know what that might be?"

Emma folded her hands and blew warm breath into them before saying, "He's upset with Melvin Shetler. The way I understand it, Melvin knew about us all along and did nothing about it. I had a wonderful childhood, but Daniel didn't fair as well."

Matthew brushed his hair back under his hat with the back of his hand. "*Jah*, he's mentioned his time in a foster home, but I don't think it was something he wanted to talk about, so I didn't press him."

"I've only heard bits and pieces, but I know something happened in one of those homes that sets him off." Emma pulled her coat tighter and headed to the door. "I'll make sure *Datt* stays inside once he comes in for the night."

"That would be great. Let's keep this between the two of us."

"*Jah.*"

Chapter 3
Forbidden

K atie stood at the mailbox at the end of her parent's driveway, sorting through a stack of mail. Emma was due any moment to go over the plans for the bakery. Only a few days had passed since her best friend's mother's funeral, and she hoped the distraction might brighten Emma's blue mood.

The snow-covered blacktop glistened in the sun as she looked toward the Byler farm expecting to catch Emma walking her way. A distant rumble forced her to step off the road just as the noise made its way over the ridge. Often, Katie's stomach did a little dance when she heard the diesel engine. Without realizing it, she instantly held her breath until she was sure it was Daniel and waved as he passed. Her acknowledgment triggered a hard brake, and she gasped as the truck fishtailed. Back under control, it backed up and stopped once it reached the mailbox.

Daniel rolled down the window, and she walked closer. He tipped the brim of his baseball cap with his finger. "Katie Yoder, you're looking mighty fine today."

Unaccustomed to compliments, Katie dropped her head to shield her color-changing cheeks. Before she had a chance to say a word, he reached over and twirled a long dark strand of hair that had escaped her full brown bonnet through his fingers.

20

Stunned by the quick exchange, she stepped back and locked her eyes on his. Not sure what to think of his flirtatious manner, she waited for an explanation.

"Is that all it takes to leave you speechless?"

"Hardly," she exclaimed quietly.

"Then why did you back away?"

"You startled me, that's all."

"I take it no guy has touched your hair before?"

He moved his finger to her cheek and then ran it over her lips. "I assume by the way your face is turning pink no one has ever done this either."

Her palms started to sweat in her gloves and her pulse quickened. "I think I should go. *Mamm* will be wondering what's taking me so long."

When she turned to leave, he let out a small whistle and then seductively hissed. "I love that wiggle."

Katie turned hard on her heel and placed one hand on her hip. "Daniel Miller, what's gotten into you today? You best keep your whistles and your hands to yourself."

"Whoa! Calm down there, girl. I was just having some fun."

"I think you best go."

Daniel took his cue to leave and waved his hand through the window leaving a trail of icy snow at her feet.

Katie stood still as he disappeared down Mystic Mill Road. Behind her, Emma hollered. "Was that Daniel?" and stopped at Katie's side.

"It was," she said as she shook her head and walked back up the driveway. "He was acting so strange. Not like himself."

Emma questioned, "Strange how?"

"I can't put my finger on it, but different. Flirtatious and almost rude."

Emma nibbled on her bottom lip, debating on how much she should share, but decided it wasn't the time and looped her arm through Katie's instead. "How about we not try to figure Daniel out, and you tell me what the bishop said to your *datt* about the bakery."

Katie squeezed Emma's hand. "I'm so excited! We finally got his permission to proceed, and *Datt* drew up some plans for us. He hopes by spring he'll have the strawberry stand converted to a working bakery."

"Oh, that's wonderful news. Just what I need. Something to look forward to."

Katie led her up the front porch steps. "I know you haven't had a minute to breathe since you got back. And I didn't want to bother you while you were taking care of your *mamm*, but we need to get this started."

"No, it's perfect. *Mamm* wouldn't want me to do anything else. She was all for us starting the bakery. Besides, Rebecca is making my life miserable at home, and I needed to get out."

"Is she still giving you a hard time?"

"*Datt* told her she's not to speak unless she has something nice to say. The quiet is worse than her sharp tongue. *Mamm* always said if she's arguing, at least you know she cares. The silent treatment is horrible. Thank goodness Anna is there as a buffer. She's the only thing keeping me from moving in with you."

"Oh Emma, it can't be that bad."

"You have no idea how hard it is to live with her."

"Suppose not, but I know her bark is worse than her bite."

~~

For the rest of the afternoon, Katie and Emma sat at the Yoder table making lists and plans of everything they needed to order before opening day. Taking the large calendar from the wall, Katie circled April thirtieth with a red marker.

"I think it's plenty of time for everything we need to do. How about you, *Datt?* Do you think you and Samuel will have it remodeled by then?"

Levi Yoder pulled on his long beard and took a seat at the table and studied their lists. "Samuel's been out there all week getting things cleaned and organized for us to start as soon as we had the bishop's approval. I think three months is plenty of time."

The clock in the living room chimed four as Emma stood to leave. "I wish I could stay longer, but I best get home to help the girls with dinner."

Ruth, Katie's *mamm*, wrapped a fresh loaf of bread and handed it to her as soon as she slipped her arms through her wool coat. With misty eyes, Ruth said, "It's your *mamm's* recipe. Don't think I'll ever be able to use another one for as long as I live."

Emma pulled Ruth in close and whispered, "You miss her as much as we do."

"For sure and certain, but it was *Gott's* will, and life goes on."

Emma held the loaf close to her chest. "But it doesn't make it any easier. *Datt* goes out to the shop every day like clockwork, but I often catch him standing on the porch or at the window staring off into space."

Levi added. "I'll be certain to stop in and check on him every few days. In times like these, we can't forget our neighbors and friends."

Emma moved to the door. "I bet he would appreciate that. None of us know what to say, and Matthew is quiet and withdrawn."

Ruth picked up the scarf and mittens off the table and handed them to Emma. "Everyone grieves in their own way, and I bet Jacob finds it easier to do it away from you *kinner*. Give him space, and he'll work his way through it. The conversations he's having with *Gott* right now will comfort him as nothing else will. *Gott* will see him through as He will Matthew and you girls."

~~

Katie stood at the sink as Emma made her way down the driveway and turned to face her parents. "She said concentrating on something else was exactly what she needed. It was nice to see her smile again."

Katie walked to where her coat hung by the back door. "I'm going to go to the strawberry stand. I want to check a few things out."

Levi cleared his throat and shook his head no. "Not yet; we want to talk to you first."

The look on her *datt's* face alarmed her. "Have I done something?"

"Not yet, but we want to get something straight," her mother added.

Levi leaned back in the chair, propped his elbows on the arms, and clasped his fingers together. "Was that Daniel Miller at the mailbox you were talking to earlier?"

"It was. He stopped for a few minutes to say hello. Is there a problem?"

"We want to make sure it doesn't become a problem," he replied.

"What do you mean?" she asked as she studied her *mamm* and then her *datt*.

"We've been hearing stories around town, and we want you to stay clear of him. He's been making a name for himself."

"Daniel and I are friends, and he's Emma's *bruder*. I can't imagine the stories are true."

In a stern voice, Levi said. "I'm not suggesting; I'm expecting you to follow our wishes. There is no reason you need to associate yourself with Daniel Miller. He's Emma's *bruder*, she has no choice, but you do."

"But *Datt*!"

"But nothing. Do you understand me? You're not to speak to him or encourage a friendship in any manner. Are we clear?"

Katie dropped her head. "Yes, sir."

He pushed his chair under the table and headed to the door. "Tell Samuel to find me when he gets back from town."

As soon as the door closed, Katie looked at her *mamm* with pleading eyes. "I don't understand the concern. What on earth did he hear in town that's so alarming that he's forbidden me to talk to him?"

Ruth walked closer to her daughter and laid her hand on her shoulder. "Your place is to obey, not question."

~~

A burst of wind circled under Emma's calf-length dress, and her thick black stockings did little to ward off the bite of winter as she walked home. A new post held up the sign at the end of the driveway, and she prayed her *datt* wouldn't ask too many questions. She went straight to the barn to find Matthew, pushing the door aside and slipping inside, out of the wind.

"Matthew, are you in here?"

"Back here."

As she followed the sound of his voice, she stopped long enough to rub the nose of Rebecca's alpaca as she passed. His whiskers tickled her hand as she stood off to the side in case he decided to spit at her gesture.

Matthew walked her way and stopped to add a scoop of grain to the bucket hung inside the stall. "What's up?"

"I was at Katie's this morning, and she mentioned Daniel stopped and talked to her. She said he was acting strange."

"Strange how?"

25

"Her exact words were 'he was flirtatious and rude.' I'm worried. And why wasn't he at work. It's the middle of the week, he should be on his delivery route."

"I saw him go by this morning, and I wondered the same thing. Maybe it's time I take a ride into town to talk to him. I think his drinking is getting out of hand."

Emma kicked a clump of straw with the toe of her black boot before saying. "My English father had a drinking problem. I sure hope Daniel isn't following in his footsteps."

Matthew rubbed between the alpaca's ears and it leaned into his touch. "Ever since the two of you got back from Sugarcreek, he hasn't been the same. Not sure what I can do, but I'll go talk to him and hope he'll open up."

Emma nuzzled the alpaca. "If he talks to anyone, it will be you, or his adoptive father."

Matthew put the lid back on the grain bin. "Now that I think of it, the last two deliveries had a different driver."

"Do you think he lost his job?" Emma asked.

"Could be."

"I sure hope not. Maybe you can get through to him."

Matthew followed her out the door. "I'll do what I can."

~~

Matthew pulled his buggy from the barn and hooked up his horse to make the short trip to town. He stretched the yellow canvas back and flipped the switch on the battery-powered heater when he heard his name.

"Matthew, I have a few more things to add to your list."

He followed the voice to the furniture shop porch, where his *datt* hollered.

"I'll be right there," he answered.

Simon, Matthew's horse, perked his ears at Matthew's voice and responded by moving the buggy forward when the leather straps tapped his back. The ice cracked under the metal wheels and Matthew pulled back on the reins, stopping right in front of the Furniture Shop.

His *datt* stepped off the porch and stopped beside the buggy. "You made some repairs to the sign."

"*Jah.*"

"I imagine one of those Englisher's were going too fast and lost control on the ice again. Not sure why they insist on driving so fast. Don't they understand they'll get more out of life if they slow down some?"

Matthew waited for more questions, hoping he could skirt around the truth if need be. When his *datt* didn't press the issue further, he took the list from his hand and guided the buggy down the frozen driveway.

The traffic on Mystic Mill Road could be challenging, especially if the snowplows didn't do a good job of clearing the snow. Matthew guided Simon up the long ridge that led to Willow Springs and prayed he'd be able to talk some sense into his best friend.

The stop sign at the crossroads of Lawrence County and Mystic Mill roads had a layer of blown snow covering it. Still, it didn't matter, since Simon instinctively stopped to give Matthew plenty of time to check for oncoming traffic. He approached the four-way stop when Daniel sped through the intersection. The buggy shook, and Simon lifted his front hoof and stomped in defiance.

Matthew pulled back on the reins. "Whoa, boy!"

His shoulders tensed, and he guided Simon to follow the black vehicle.

"He's going to kill himself, if not someone else," he thought.

There was no way he'd catch up with him, but he kept scanning the businesses along the way to be sure he had not made a stop. As he reached Rt. 208, he saw a circle of trucks in an open parking lot all positioned around a massive bonfire. The afternoon temperatures were falling, and he was surprised the group was gathering in the cold.

Without giving the consequences any thought, he pulled into the lot and found a nearby tree to secure Simon.

A loud voice carried in the wind. "Matthew, over here."

The gust tipped his wool hat up, and he grabbed the brim and pulled it down tighter. He followed Daniel's voice to the fire.

Daniel tossed a can of beer his way, catching the cold aluminum in his bare hands. Matthew threw it back in one quick move.

"None for me, thanks."

"Come on man, lighten up. Your old man isn't here to watch you. Technically, you're still on your *Rumspringa.* No one will be the wiser if you tip one *back with me."

Matthew listened as Daniel's friends egged him on.

Someone hollered across the fire. "What's up? Is your holier than thou friend too good to drink with us?"

Daniel yelled back, "Give the man a break; he just got here."

Matthew moved closer and held out his bare hands over the fire. Lowering his voice and without looking away, he asked through gritted teeth. "What are you doing?"

"What does it look like I'm doing?" Daniel said as he held up a can of beer to the group of men on the other side of the fire. "I'm having some fun with friends."

"I'd say your new group of friends aren't the best influence right now." He stopped and let the fire warm him and moved closer to Daniel's side. "Look, don't you realize you become who you surround yourself with?"

Daniel didn't respond but tipped his head back to finish the beer before tossing the empty can in the back of his truck.

"Loads of good that's done me in the past."

"What's that supposed to mean?"

"I've surrounded myself with the likes of you for the last seven years, and where did that get me?"

"Where did you expect to be?"

"Anywhere but stuck in Willow Springs without a job."

"What happened with that?"

"Long story, but my boss didn't think eleven o'clock was a good start time. I personally think eleven is the perfect time to start with a hangover."

Matthew stuffed his hands in his pockets. "Emma is worried about you."

"Well, you can tell Miss Emma her big brother is fine. Besides, if I had any say about it, I'd wrench her off that farm. She needs to experience life in the real world."

Matthew grabbed him by the arm. "I'd think twice about that if I were you."

Daniel pulled his arm from his grip and doubled his fist, stopping short of Matthew's chin. "What you seem to forget is she's more my sister than yours."

Matthew looked him square in the eye. "She has no desire to leave, or she'd have done so by now."

"She doesn't know any better. Your father has kept her shielded in his little fantasy world for the last sixteen years. My own father had it right."

Matthew stopped and tried to think of what he knew about Daniel's biological father. All he knew is he left the Amish, became an alcoholic and treated his mother poorly. When he remembered, he asked, "How can anything your father did come into play?"

"He left the Amish because there were too many rules, and he couldn't live up to the expectations of his father."

Letting out a long sigh Matthew repositioned his hat on his head and asked, "What does that have to do with Emma?"

"All she has known is rules and how to be a respectable Amish girl. She needs to learn that life doesn't revolve around rules a bunch of elders and bishops put together to follow."

Matthew didn't flinch. "I wouldn't go there."

Daniel closed the distance between them, the brims of their hats touching and asked through clenched teeth. "What are you going to do about it?"

Matthew turned and walked away.

"That's what I thought."

Chapter 4

Singeon

Emma pressed the wrinkles out of her black dress and yearned to wear her pretty blue one instead. She desperately missed her *mamm*, but no amount of black could fill the emptiness in her heart.

It took Katie some convincing to get her to attend the Sunday night *singeon*. She only agreed after Samuel offered to drive them. With the Kaufman farm being two miles away, she didn't relish walking in the cold. It'd been six months since any part of her felt like attending a youth gathering, but a tiny part of her looked forward to seeing her friends.

Samuel had been more than patient with her over the last year, and she was confident he would be expecting to drive her home. There wasn't an ounce of doubt that she desired the same thing. They had been friends since they were toddlers, and their hearts had been intertwined seriously for more years than they could count. She might only be sixteen and still too young for any talk of marriage, but Samuel was the one she planned to spend her life with.

A soft knock on her bedroom door averted her attention away from Samuel when Anna pushed open the door. "*Datt* is letting Rebecca and I drive the family buggy to the *singeon*. Are you riding with us?"

Laying her brush back on the nightstand, Emma asked, "Isn't Matthew going?"

"I don't think so. He's been in a foul mood for days and said a youth gathering is the last place he wants to be."

Emma knew exactly what Matthew's problem was, but she wasn't about to share that with Anna. If he's not going, why are you taking the family buggy? Wouldn't it be easier to take Matthews courting buggy? It's much smaller and easier to handle."

"He left an hour or so ago and said he wouldn't be back in time for us to use it. Between you and me, I think he's meeting Sarah Mast."

"What makes you think that?"

" Only a boy who was meeting a girl would put a clean shirt on."

Emma giggled as she twisted her hair back up in a bun at the nape of her neck. "I suppose you're right. I hope it works out with him and Sarah. They've been waiting a long time."

"Me too. He thinks we all don't know, but I see how he looks at her."

Re-adjusting the straight pins that held her *kapp* on, Emma added. "I don't think he's talked to another girl in the *g'may* in years, and I know *Datt* is anxious for him to take his kneeling vow. He keeps asking him about it. I think the only thing that is holding him back is waiting on Sarah."

Anna sat on the edge of Emma's bed. "He'll be twenty-three in a few weeks, and it's high time he finds himself a *fraa* and settles down. Besides, Rebecca and I are already arguing who'll get his room once he leaves."

Emma took a seat beside her. "Counting your chickens before they hatch, don't you think?"

"I suppose so, but you never had to share a room with Rebecca."

Emma stood to go downstairs. "*Gott* willing, I never will."

"I heard that," Rebecca snapped.

Emma didn't deny her comment but smiled and tried to lighten the mood when they met her in the hallway. "You must agree you wouldn't want to share a room with me either."

"For sure and certain," Rebecca snarled.

"You didn't answer me," Anna asked. "Are you going with us?"

"No, I'm riding with Samuel and Katie. They should be here any minute."

~~

The moon glistened off the snow-covered ground as Emma stood on the porch waiting for Samuel and Katie. After checking on her *datt* and warming up his coffee, he assured her he'd be okay if she left. The lump that formed in the back of her throat had yet to disappear when she noticed his eyes mist over as he looked at the empty chair beside him. It would be the first time since the funeral he had been alone, and she got the feeling he was looking forward to a few hours to himself.

Emma looked toward the sound of the approaching buggy while rubbing her mittened hands together. When it pulled up beside her, she waved a friendly hello and walked to the buggy's opposite side. Before she had a chance to climb inside, Samuel handed the reins over to his *schwester* and was at Emma's side helping her up on the bench seat. The buggy, only meant for two, left the three of them snuggling in close. She wondered why he didn't think to bring a larger one; however, she didn't mind the closeness to keep warm. Hot bricks had been wrapped in weighty towels and placed on the floorboard to keep their feet warm, and Samuel had added a couple of thick blankets to cover their lap.

Once they made it to the Kaufman's on Willow Creek Road, Samuel dropped them off at the barn entrance. The girls stepped down, and once Samuel had pulled away, Katie reached for Emma's arm to tug her aside before they stepped inside. The door was ajar, and the lanterns' soft glow gave Emma enough light to take note of the worry lines etched on Katie's face.

"What is it? You were awful quiet on the ride here."

"I've been dying to talk to you for days, but *Mamm* had me so busy I didn't have a chance to walk over and see you."

"You're worrying me. What's the matter?" Emma asked.

"My parents forbid me to talk to Daniel. They fear he's a bad influence."

"Why on earth would they think that?"

"I'm not sure. *Datt* said he heard something in town he didn't like. He wouldn't tell me what it was, only that I needed to obey him."

"Oh my, that's terrible. What are we going to do?"

"I'm not sure. Do you have any idea what my parents heard? They won't share it with me."

Emma looked over her shoulder to be sure no one was in earshot and mouthed. "He's been drinking a lot."

"That's it!" Katie exclaimed.

"What's that?"

"Why he was acting so strange the other day. He was very forward with me, and it made me uncomfortable. I never felt that way around him before."

Pulling Katie inside and out of the cold, Emma tilted closer. "Matthew had a run-in with him the other day as well. He wouldn't tell me what it was about, but he's been in a foul mood ever since."

Katie waved to a group of their friends and whispered, "I don't care what my *datt* says, he needs his friends more than ever, and I'm not turning my back on him."

Emma grabbed her arm. "You must conform to your parents. What if they find out? They'll forbid you from seeing me, and I would die if that happened."

Katie took Emma's hand and led her across the room to where their friends gathered on benches. "Don't you worry about that; I'll deal with my parents. I'm more concerned with turning my back on Daniel if he needs his friends now."

Katie stopped in the middle of the room and turned to Emma. "Do you still have the phone Daniel gave you last summer?"

"*Jah*. Why?"

"Maybe I could use it to call him?"

Emma hesitated. "I'm not so sure that's a good idea. It hasn't been charged in months. For all I know, it might not even work. I don't know if he kept it activated."

Katie slipped her arms out of her coat. "I highly doubt that. It was his only connection to you for a long time, so I bet he kept it turned on."

"How will you charge it?"

"Let me borrow it and I'll find a way."

Emma furrowed her eyebrows together and lightly pushed her friend ahead of her. "I'll think about it."

Emma moved the songbook from the bench to her lap and slid down so Katie could sit beside her. Katie fell into conversation with the two girls to her left, and she looked around the room for Samuel. When she caught his eye from across the room, he tipped his hat and motioned for her to meet him at the snack table. She excused herself from the circle of girls and made her way across the room.

Samuel handed her a cup of punch and moved in close enough to quietly ask, "May I take you home tonight?"

The paper cup shook slightly at the exchange. "I would assume since you brought me."

"No, I mean alone, without Katie tagging along. I'll find someone to give her a ride if you agree."

35

The smile on his face told her he had not given up on them. "I'd like that."

The slow and steady voices behind them led them both back to their friends.

Not needing the hymn book, her voice melted in with the others as they sang *Amazing Grace*. The words made a beautiful sound, and Emma smiled with the thought of picking things up with Samuel where they left off six months earlier. She scanned the room and found him propped up against an empty stall, looking her way. Daydreaming for a few seconds about what it would be like to spend the rest of her life with him, she thought. *Was it too early to be thinking such things?* So much had happened, and so many things still needed to be sorted out. Was she really ready for any of that? All of a sudden, an unnerving amount of pressure built up in her chest, and she let out a long sigh.

Katie elbowed her. "Is something the matter?"

They had been best friends since they were children, and if anyone was going to notice a change in her demeanor, it would be Katie.

"I'll be right back. I need some fresh air."

An uneasiness crept up the back of her neck as she weaved her way to the door. When she opened it, a blast of air circled her face, forcing her to pull her brown bonnet tighter under her chin. Taking mittens from her pockets, she found comfort in their softness and pulled her black coat tighter around her middle. The sharpness in the air filled her lungs as she tried to clear her mind. She knew what Samuel wanted, and at one point, she was sure she wanted that as well. Now, after everything, was she ready to give Samuel what was clearly written on his face? If she was honest with herself, the answer would be ... *no*.

She made her way to the white picket fence at the side of the barn and rested her arms on the top rail. Closing her eyes, she raised her head to the blackened sky and prayed.

"Heavenly Father, please give me peace. I feel restless and anxious and know you are the only one I can find assurance in. I think Samuel is ready to move to the next step, but I don't want to rush your plans. Is that what you want me to do? Help me see your hand in all of this. And please help me find a way to help Daniel. He's hurting and angry. What do you want us both to learn through all of this? I'm so confused. Please fill me with your presence, so I know what path to take. Your will, not mine. Amen."

The beautiful voices from inside the barn added a magical feel to the stillness in the air. She continued to keep her eyes closed while absorbing the sound. When she succumbed to the cold, the light from the lanterns seeped out from underneath the wooden doors led her back inside. A few propane heaters had been added throughout the open space to add warmth to the drafty area. For the next forty-five minutes, the singing continued, and Emma enjoyed the fellowship and praise through song.

~~

For Samuel, his time had finally arrived. Emma was across the room, and there was a lightness in his heart that warmed every time he looked her way. For the last five years, he waited for her to be old enough, and now on the cusp of her agreeing to let him take her home, his dreams were coming true. He was more than ready to commit himself to the church and Emma. His only concern was if she would be willing to go against tradition and take her kneeling vow early? The bishop approved a young marriage before, and he saw no problem in him doing it again. Things were finally falling in place. With the plans that Katie and Emma were making to build the bakery, he was certain his *datt* would agree to let him build a house next to the strawberry fields.

His mind was swimming with all the plans, and he couldn't wait to start sharing them with Emma. Once the singing stopped, he waited for her to look his way. Motioning his head in the direction of the buggy, he silently told her he would meet her outside. He secured a ride home for Katie with Rebecca and Anna and said his goodbyes to his friends.

~~

Katie gathered up her gloves and scarf off the bench and asked. "I assume if Samuel handed me off to your *schwesters,* he has plans for the two of you tonight?"

Without looking to her friend, Emma said in a long, drawn-out sigh, *"Jah."*

"You don't sound very excited."

She pulled Katie back down on the bench. "What am I going to do?"

"What do you mean? I thought you'd be excited."

"I don't think I'm ready for what he has in mind."

"Well, tell him that. He'll understand. I'm sure of it."

"I'm not too sure about that. He's already waited so long and remember he's three years older than me. He might be ready to settle down, but I'm far from it."

"If he cares about you, he'll wait. Be honest with him."

"What if I'm never ready?"

"What do you mean if you're never ready?"

"I have so many questions about committing to this way of life."

Scrunching together her eyebrows, Katie asked, "You can't be serious?"

"Oh, please don't tell anyone I said that. I'm just so confused."

"No one said you need to marry him today or make any decisions about your life. We're sixteen and way too young to even be thinking about that. I can't imagine what's on his mind, other than wanting to court you."

"Perhaps so."

Katie positioned her heavy brown bonnet over her starched white *kapp* and asked, "Do you think you're ready for that?"

"I don't think so. I thought that's what I wanted, but now I'm not sure."

"You need to take it to *Gott* before you commit to anything."

"I already did, and I hope He'll give me some clarity about it. I've been trying to figure it out on my own all evening. I'm sure Samuel will understand if I want to think about things for a while. That will give me time to wait on *Gott* with my concerns."

Katie stood to leave. "I best go find your *schwesters* before I lose my way home and have to walk in the cold."

"Thanks, Katie, you're a wonderful friend. What would I do without you?"

Katie patted the back of her hand. "Be truthful with him. As my *mamm* says, "Honesty is always the best policy.""

~~

Emma stood outside the barn for a moment, waiting for her eyes to adjust to the dark as she located Samuel. It was evident couples were pairing off and disappearing in the confines of enclosed buggies. Samuel waved her over and stood holding the canvas aside, so she could crawl inside. Without saying a word, she covered her lap with the wool blanket while he took his place behind the reins.

"Are you warm enough?"

She tucked the blanket under her thighs and said, *"Jah."*

He clicked his tongue, speaking to his horse in a language only the two of them understood, and the buggy moved forward.

39

Emma glanced over at him, and even though the darkness shielded his face, she sensed he was smiling. The clip-clop of the horses' hooves added a steady beat to the snow-packed road before he spoke. "I've been waiting a long time for this night. We have so much to talk about."

She twisted her mitten-covered hands on her lap but didn't respond.

"I thought we'd stop beside Willow Creek for a little bit before I take you home."

She had never heard Samuel talk so much, and while she was struggling to keep the nervousness in her stomach at bay, he filled the space with conversation.

She was enjoying listening to him, and there was no doubt she was attracted to him. In her head, she played over the sweet things he'd done and said to her over the years. The way he teased her and looked out for her. The way he tied yellow ribbons to the chicken coop just for her and especially giving her Someday. The dog had become the best present and reminded her daily how he felt. Even the way he called her "*My Emma*" played in her head. For months leading up to her sixteenth birthday, she could think of nothing else but being old enough to attend her first *singeon* and accepting a ride home from him. But Daniel, her mother, and losing her *mamm* changed her life. She silently prayed again, *"Oh, Gott, help me find the words to explain without hurting his feelings."*

As the buggy came to a stop at a clearing before the covered bridge, Emma took in a long breath and prepared herself for what Samuel had to say.

He clicked on the battery-operated flashlight that sat on the floor and twisted to her. Gathering her hands in his. He removed her mittens and rubbed her chilled fingers between his own and rested his forehead on hers.

His breath tickled her nose. "You have no idea how long I've waited for this night." He let his lips rest on her cheek and continued.

40

"I close my eyes, and you're there, I wake, and you're there, I breathe, and you're there."

She let the warmth of his calloused hands rest inside of hers for only a few seconds before she pulled away.

"What's the matter?"

She tucked her hands back in her mittens. "I want to explain a few things."

"What is there to explain? I'm here, you're here; it's what we've been planning on for years."

She backed away from his hold. "Just let me talk. "

"Okay."

"I think you want things that I'm not too sure I'm ready for yet."

Samuel shifted on the bench and waited for her to continue.

"I don't know how to say this other than to just spit it out."

"I'm listening."

Her voice cracked. "I'm not ready for all of this."

In an instant, the softness she saw in his eyes turned cold. "I thought it's what we both wanted. You have a lot going on right now, but I thought we could face them together as we start to make plans for our future."

In a wistful tone, he continued, "You're only sixteen, but the bishop's approved young marriages before, and I'm sure he'll do it again."

Emma fidgeted in her seat. "Marriage? That's the farthest from my mind. I thought you wanted to start courting. I had no idea you were anticipating marriage."

He moved closer and picked up her covered hands, then removed her mittens again. "Look, I might be moving too fast, and I'm sorry about that. I've been thinking about you and our life for years now. My thoughts may be ahead of yours, but at this point, I'll be content with courting."

41

"I'm not ready to even commit to that at this point. It wouldn't be fair of me to promise you something I'm not sure of myself."

"What are you saying?"

Squeezing his fingertips, she said, "I'm trying to say that I don't want to hold you back."

"Hold me back from what?"

"From settling down and starting a family. Even from joining the church."

He lifted her hands to his lips. "All of those things …I want to do with you."

Emma sighed, "I'm not ready to start thinking about that. I just started my *Rumspringa,* and there is so much of life I want to think about before I commit to you or anyone else."

Samuel's tone hardened. "What about the plans with Katie and the bakery? And besides, you're saying no before you even give yourself time to think about it. Don't you think you could think about it for a while first?"

"I'm not saying I'm leaving Willow Springs or giving up on the bakery. I'm saying I don't think I'm old enough to make you any promises."

He paused, and his shoulders dropped. "I guess it's been this long. I can wait a little longer."

She pulled her hands away, tucked the blanket back under her thighs, and took a second to weigh her words. "I can't ask you to do that. It wouldn't be fair."

He sat up straighter and took in a deep breath. "Don't you think that's for me to decide?"

"How can I ask you to wait on me if I'm not sure what my future holds? I don't want to feel obligated or watch you wait for something I'm so unsure about."

Pools of tears started to form, the immensity of what she was suggesting sank in. "It wouldn't be fair. Don't put your life on hold because of me."

"You don't understand. I don't want a life with anyone else. I only want it with you."

"Samuel, please don't make this harder than it already is. I can't give you what you desire ...and I'm not sure I ever will."

He pulled her closer and tenderly pressed his lips against hers. The saltiness from her tears mixed with his warm breath, and he whispered, "I'll give you time. I pushed too fast. I'm sorry. I'll wait."

She put her hand on his chest and struggled through a sniffle. "No, please don't. I can't ask you to do that. It's too much. I can't make you any promises."

He reached down, turned off the light, and picked up the reins.

Chapter 5
Cover of Darkness

Katie smiled at Emma when she climbed up in her *bruder's* buggy. This was the start of Emma becoming her *schwester-in-law*. She was sure of it, even if Emma wasn't certain herself. She couldn't contain all the happy thoughts conjuring up in her head about finally having a *schwester* to share life with.

She scanned the driveway looking to locate Rebecca and Anna's buggy and heard her name in the darkness.

"Katie, over here."

The moon bounced a shadow off the snow-covered ground near the trees next to the wooden structure. She followed the voice into the blackness.

Daniel stood rubbing his hands together and blowing into his cupped hands. "I've been waiting here for over an hour to get you. Let me drive you home. I want to talk to you."

She looked over her shoulder to be certain no one saw them. "Rebecca and Anna are waiting for me. I'm not sure what to tell them. And besides, I'm not allowed to see you. My *datt* will be furious if he finds out."

Daniel pulled her into the shadows as a group of teenagers passed by. "They won't ask any questions if you tell them you've accepted a ride home. Will they? As far as your dad is concerned, what he doesn't know won't hurt."

"No, I suppose not."

"Perfect. Walk to the road, and I'll pick you up."

Before twisting to leave, she said, "I won't be getting in unless there is no one around."

"Alright already, just go!"

Every ounce of her body shook with excitement as she went to find Rebecca. She zigzagged her way to the center of buggies and prayed the night sky would hide the lie she was about to tell. She wondered, *Was it really a fib or more of a stretch of the truth? No matter how she looked at it, she was getting a ride home, just not with an acceptable boy.*

She took in a deep breath and reached out to touch the back of Rebecca's coat. "I won't be needing a ride home after all."

Without even seeing the outline of Rebecca's mouth, her voice held a teasing tone. "Well, now isn't that the talk of the town. I wonder who the lucky fellow might be. Could it be one of the Kaufman boys, or perhaps Eli Bricker's cousin who's visiting from Lancaster?"

Katie laid her hand across her friend's arm and coyly said, "Now, you know as well as I do, I'll never tell."

Anna piped in. "Silly secrets, I'm dying to know who it is, and you can be sure Rebecca and I will be trying to figure it out all the way home."

Glad the blackened sky hid most of her face, Katie waved to them both and disappeared into the night.

Hiding in the shadow of the barn while the last of the buggies pulled away, she rubbed her mittens together and pulled her bonnet tighter around her chin. For a split second, her *datt's* warning played over in her head. The guilt of disobeying him left a heaviness in her chest. The sound of a distant owl and the scurry of a nighttime rodent played a song as she walked down the snow-covered drive. The familiar sound of Daniel's engine crested the hill on Willow Creek Road long before its headlights made it to her side.

The passenger side door flew open as soon as it came to a stop. She crawled inside and held her fingers over the heat in the dashboard. "I lied to Rebecca and Anna, and I don't like doing that."

Daniel pulled back out to the center of the road and asked, "Do you want to go to the Sandwich Shoppe? I'll buy us some hot chocolate."

She'd love something warm to drink, but there was no way she could chance anyone seeing them together. "We'd better not. I wouldn't want any of *Datt's* friends to catch me in public with you."

Creasing his forehead, he asked, "Why not?"

Katie closed her hands on her lap. "Let's just say you're off-limits."

"Off-limits? What's that supposed to mean?"

"My parents don't want us to be friends."

"Why not? I've never had any trouble with your dad before."

By the pitch in his voice, Katie weighed her words. "You know how parents can be, sometimes."

"No, I don't. Why don't you explain it to me?"

"I'm Amish. You're English."

Daniel's voice raised an octave. "Didn't seem to matter last summer when they needed help with Samuel's deliveries, now did it?"

The tension in the air created an uncomfortable silence, and she tried to lighten the mood. "I'm their only daughter, so I'm sure they're being overprotective. I'm sure it's nothing, and I wouldn't worry about it."

"If you're not worried about it, then I say we go for hot chocolate."

Still unsure it was the right thing to do, she conceded. "Okay."

He parked the truck in front of the Sandwich Shoppe on Main Street and instructed her to stay put until he came around to open her door.

She took advantage of the few seconds alone to look around the lighted street. She prayed she wouldn't see anyone who recognized her.

As they made their way to the door, he held it open, and a wave of coffee and fresh bread filled her senses when she stepped inside. She scanned the room but didn't recognize anyone who might concern her.

Daniel guided her to the counter. "Would you like anything besides hot chocolate?"

"No, I think that will hit the spot."

"Good, how about you find us a table, and I'll be right with you."

Katie turned to locate a table with a full view of the door but secluded from the large front windows, just as Matthew and Sarah walked inside. Her heart skipped a beat when Sarah raised her hand and walked her way.

"Katie Yoder, nice to see you. Who are you here with?"

Without letting her answer, Sarah examined the tables and pointed across the room. "We could sit together."

Matthew tipped his hat to Katie and smiled.

Distress lodged in her throat as she waited for them both to realize who she was with. The smile disappeared on Matthew's face as soon as Daniel walked up behind her.

Matthew removed his hat. "Daniel."

Daniel motioned his head toward the table and responded abruptly. "Matthew."

Their icy glare left Katie wishing she'd gone home with the Byler twins as she took the mug of hot chocolate from his hand and sat it on the table in front of her. She removed her bonnet and slipped her arms out of her wool coat. Sarah's chatter outweighed their chilled exchange as she persistently plummeted them with questions, not giving either one of them a chance to answer.

Sarah pointed to Katie's cup. "Matthew, I think their hot chocolate looks yummy. I'll have the same, but I'd like mine with whipped topping."

Katie held the cup to her mouth, hoping Sarah would continue to monopolize the conversation. Not realizing she was suddenly holding her breath, she released it, splashing cocoa down the side of the mug.

Daniel moved in closer. "I need to talk to Matthew for a minute. Do you need anything else?"

"A napkin?"

"Will do. I'll be right back."

With both men away from the table, Sarah leaned in and asked, "You and Daniel?"

Katie dropped her eyes. "It's not what you think. We're just friends."

Sarah slipped her coat down past her shoulders and removed her brown bonnet. "Out on a Sunday evening might indicate otherwise."

"I promise you it's not what it seems."

Leaning in close, Sarah added. "He's quite handsome. Don't you think?"

A wave of warmth colored Katie's cheeks. "I hadn't much noticed."

"Oh, come on, Katie, any girl with good eyesight would find it hard not to be attracted to Daniel Miller."

Katie twisted her *kapp* string between her fingers and peeked over her shoulder before turning back to Sarah. "But he's English, and you know as well as I do that wouldn't sit well with my parents or the bishop."

"He might be English, but the way I understand it, his roots dig deep into the Amish."

"True. Nevertheless, I'm not too sure I want to be seen with him. My *datt* will not be happy if he finds out."

Sarah looked around the restaurant and patted her forearm. "By the looks of it, there isn't anyone here you need to worry about, and Matthew and I won't say a word."

"Thank you."

Sarah twisted in her chair. "I wonder what's taking Matthew so long?"

"Where did they go?" Sarah asked as she glanced around the room.

~~

Daniel walked past Matthew and waved his hand, instructing him to follow him out the back entrance. He pushed the door open and turned to face Matthew. "I owe you an apology. I'm not sure what got into me the other night."

Matthew rested against the railing and crossed his arms over his chest. "I know exactly what got into you, and it had a lot to do with the beer cans you were chucking in the back of your truck."

Daniel put his hands in his jean pockets. "So? I had a few beers, the last time I checked it isn't a crime."

"It is if you use them to take whatever's eating you out on your friends."

"I was having some fun with you, that's all."

"It was more than just having some fun. You challenged me to fight you."

"I was just messing with you."

"Regardless, I didn't appreciate it."

Daniel reached his hand out. "Friends?"

Matthew took a few moments before returning the gesture. "Good enough friends that you'll take some advice?"

"What's that?"

"Find a way to get that chip off your shoulder before you push the few friends you have in this town away."

"What makes you think I have anything I'm holding on to?"

"Because the Daniel I know would never raise a fist to me. Or wouldn't think twice about treating Katie with anything but respect. Emma mentioned you treated her harshly the other day."

Daniel shifted his weight to his other foot. "I plan on apologizing."

"You should, and you should also know word around town is you're raising Cain with your new group of friends."

"Leave it to the Amish grapevine to tangle me up in their gossip."

"Gossip or not, you can guarantee Levi Yoder isn't going to be happy you're out with his daughter."

Daniel flipped up the collar of his leather jacket. "Well, he can get in line right behind my grandfather if he thinks his opinion matters much."

"That's the chip I'm talking about."

"So, I'm holding a grudge toward the old man. Nothing a stiff drink won't fix."

Matthew stepped his foot in front of the door as Daniel laid his hand on the knob. "Not around Katie."

Daniel forced the door open harder. "What do you think I am? A moron?"

~~

"There you are. Where did you go? Sarah asked.

Matthew pulled a chair out next to her. "We stepped outside for a minute. Are you ladies all caught up?"

Sarah winked at Katie. "We sure are."

"Matthew tells me you and Emma are going to open a bakery together. I think that's a great idea. Do you have any idea when that might happen?"

"*Datt* says they'll have everything ready about the same time the strawberries come in. We hope to offer fresh strawberry pies and fry pies along with donuts and bread. They're working on laying out the kitchen right now. I'm excited, and I think Emma is too."

Sarah took a sip of her hot chocolate before saying, "Emma needs something to keep her busy. When my *mamm* died, it helped when I was too busy to think about how much I missed her."

"For sure and certain," Katie replied.

Katie pushed her cup to the middle of the table. "Daniel, I better go home."

"So soon?" Sarah asked.

Katie stood, put her coat and bonnet on, and rested her hand on Sarah's shoulder. "I'm sure you and Matthew have plenty to talk about, and you don't need us interrupting your time together."

"I guess so, but it was nice to visit with you. I'm working at my *datt's* lumber mill, so I'm busy most days, but let's find some time to visit again real soon."

Katie headed to the door. "I'd like that."

Matthew nodded in Daniel's direction without saying a word.

~~

A burst of wind swirled under Katie's skirt as they stepped out on the sidewalk. "Burr, where did that come from?"

Daniel hurried toward the door and helped her in before climbing inside himself. He wasted no time revving the engine and turning up the heat. "Give it a couple of minutes, it will warm up quickly."

Katie held her hands up to the heater vent. "I could get used to this."

51

Daniel pulled out into traffic, took the first right at the light, and pulled into the empty parking lot behind the row of brick buildings on Main Street. After shifting to park, he said, "Before I take you home, I have a few things to say."

Katie gathered her hands in her lap and waited.

He turned in his seat to face her. "I hear I was rude the other day."

Katie didn't know what to say and took a few seconds before responding. "Not rude as much as different. You've never spoken to me like that, so it caught me off guard. I suppose Emma told you it made me uncomfortable?"

"In a roundabout way. Emma must have said something to Matthew, and he called me out on it. For whatever it's worth, I'm sorry. I don't know what got into me."

"I don't either, but let's just say your apology is accepted. Consider it forgotten."

As he pulled away, he asked, "So, tell me about your bakery plans. What are you calling it?"

A small giggle escaped her lips before saying, "Emma and I are at odds about the name. We can't decide if it should be "Katie and Emma's Sweet Shoppe" or "Emma and Katie's."

"If I had a vote, I'd say Katie and Emma's."

Curious, she asked, "Why's that?"

"Let's say I'm a bit partial to the name Katie."

A flutter filled Katie's stomach. "So, you know other Katie's?"

"Nope, just one."

For a few minutes, Katie let his words sink in as she tried not to read too much into his comment. It was hard not to hear the softness in his voice when he said her name. Who was she trying to kid? Daniel Miller wouldn't be interested in her, would he?

As they got closer to her *haus*, he flipped off the lights and drove in darkness as they approached her driveway.

"Oh, thank you. I worried my parents might see you drop me off. No need stirring up trouble about nothing."

He pulled to the end of her driveway and stopped. "Wait, let me shut off the cab light before you open the door."

Flipping the switch to his right, he said, "There you go, you're all set. No one will be the wiser you hitched a ride with an Englisher."

"Hitch a ride? I'd say you didn't give me much chance to tell you no."

"I guess you're right. I was going to get you alone for a few minutes even if I had to pick you up and carry you over my shoulder."

"You wouldn't dare!"

"If it was the only way to get you to go with me, you can bet your bottom dollar I would've."

As she reached for the door handle, he locked it under her fingers. "Now, how do you expect me to go home if you lock me in?"

"Maybe I'm not ready to let you go yet."

"Daniel, I should get home. I bet *Mamm* is pacing the floor."

He reached out and laid his fingers on her knee, making small circles through her dark blue dress. "Where is the next youth gathering?"

"Why?"

"I want to go."

"But why?"

"Could be I find a young Amish girl interesting."

Under the cover of the night sky, she was glad he didn't see her blush as she teased back. "Who could that be? Maybe one of the Byler twins? They're about your age. Or how about Edna Graber. I hear she's dated a few English boys."

"Nope, none of them. But I bet you'd find out if you tell me when and where the next party is."

53

"You know as well as I do, they're not parties. Just snacks and singing."

He smirked. "Some good old fashion matchmaking, as well, I'm sure of it."

"That too, but I wouldn't know anything about that. I've only been going for about six months. She pulled the lock up and reached for the door handle. Again, he pressed the button to lower the lock.

"You didn't answer me. Where is the next one?"

"Here, but I don't think it's a good idea for you to come. *Datt* would never allow it."

"We'll see about that. You let me worry about him."

He finally let her open the door, and before she had a chance to close it behind her, he said, "By the way, I think you're worth stirring up trouble."

She closed the door and let him pull away. He was at least five hundred feet down the road before she saw his lights come back on. The cold air did little to cool the heat that rose to her face as she played his words over in her head. No matter how hard she tried to ignore it, there was something about Daniel Miller that tied her stomach in knots and left her breathless. How was she ever going to face her parents? Better yet, how would she face the fact that she was falling for a boy off-limits in her world?

Chapter 6
Memories

Emma stood at the mailbox, sorting through the stack of cards and letters still coming in with condolences. The daily reminder left an emptiness etched deep inside. In the two weeks since she told Samuel she didn't want him to wait for her, tears continued to teeter on her bottom lashes. Between the tension with Rebecca, Daniel's drinking, and now pushing Samuel away, a dark cloud encircled her.

Marie's familiar handwriting made her tuck the remaining bundle under her arm and gingerly slid her finger under the flap.

My Dearest Elizabeth,

I should address you as Emma, but you'll always be my Elizabeth, so please forgive me if I can't bring myself to address you by Emma all the time.

Amos is down for a nap, and Rachel is in school, so I wanted to take a few minutes to write you. It's been quite chilly here, and with it getting dark so early, I've been spending a lot of time with Nathan and the children learning to speak Dutch. Even Rosie is trying to help. Yesterday they all decided to a no-English day. It was quite comical trying to understand what they were saying, but I think it helped. I've also been meeting with some of the elders, and hopefully, by springtime, I'll be to a point where I can join the church.

While I enjoy my alone time at night, it will be nice when Nathan and I can marry, and I can move into his house. I thank the Lord every day he brought me here and that Daniel was able to find you. For so many years, I felt lost and alone, but you and Nathan showed me I'm not alone and can come back from so much pain.

Every time I think of you or Daniel, I say a little prayer that things are going well for you. I can only imagine you are missing Stella and wish I was closer to fill the void more.

I'm not sure why, but Daniel's weighed heavy on my mind. Please write me back and let me know how things are going for him. He was so angry at your mother's funeral. I'm so worried about him, and your grandfather is concerned as well. He stopped by this morning and asked my opinion about coming to see you both. He so desperately wants to restore that relationship. How do you feel about that? I'm not sure Daniel is ready yet. When I look into Daniel's eyes, I see your father, Jake. It's the same look he had when he spoke of Melvin. Unfortunately for your grandfather, Daniel's anger is so evident that he's getting the brunt of it once again from his grandson. I feel bad for him, and even though I disagree with how he handled things, I see the pain in his eyes. I can't help but feel compassion toward him.

I've given a lot of thought to what he did, and I believe God would want all three of us to forgive him. He only did what he thought was best for all of us at the time. How can we get Daniel to see that?

All my love,
Momma

Emma creased the yellow lined paper and secured it back into its envelope as she walked to the *haus*. Before she wrote to her mother, she needed to talk to Daniel. Dropping the mail in the basket on the counter, she headed to her room. Hidden in a shoebox inside her hope chest, she retrieved the cell phone Daniel had given her last summer.

On the floor, she prayed it had enough charge she could make one quick call. She pressed the power button, it chimed, and she buried it between her knees to muffle the sound. Her *schwesters* were in the basement doing laundry, but she didn't want to take any chances.

She moved to the window, held it to the light, eager for the small solid battery bar to appear. Tilting her ear toward the door, she tapped on Daniel's picture. On the second ring, he answered.

"Emma?"

"Listen, I don't have much battery. Can you meet me at the covered bridge in thirty minutes?"

"Is something the matter?"

"I'll explain when I see you."

She barely got the last word out before the phone powered down automatically.

Before tucking it back in its hiding place, she decided to put it in her pocket in hopes of charging it in Daniel's truck. Katie's request played in her head as she toyed with the idea of letting her use it. If she or Matthew couldn't get through to Daniel, maybe Katie could. The steps creaked under her feet as she made her way back downstairs. Tiptoeing to the back door, she slipped on her boots and coat before heading outside. If the girls heard her leave, she'd never be able to sneak out without hearing Rebecca's wrath for not helping with the mounds of laundry that had built up.

The sun was shining bright, but it did little to ward off the wind whipping around the house. It had been too cold to add snow to the frozen ground, and for that, she was grateful. Had the snow been deep, she wouldn't be able to make it down the lane that ran the line of trees that separated the Byler and Yoder farms. It was the quickest way to make it to the covered bridge that canopied Willow Creek. The trees, barren of leaves, did little to keep her hidden, and she prayed everyone was too busy to pay her any mind.

Once she made it to the back of the property and followed the creek path, she slowed her steps and breathed a sigh of relief when she noticed Daniel parked in the clearing right before the bridge. She waved in his direction as she rounded the bend. He had the engine idling and leaned over and pushed her door open from the inside.

"Thanks for meeting me on such short notice."

"Not a problem. What's up?"

Emma held her hands over the vent. "I got a letter from Marie today."

"Oh yeah, what did she have to say?"

"Melvin wants to visit."

"Hell, NO!

Emma snapped her head in his direction. "Daniel!"

"He's the last person I want to see."

"Don't you think you could give him a chance to explain?"

His knuckles turned white as he grasped the steering wheel. "He had his chance, and he gave that up when he made me a ward of the state."

She pushed the creases out of her dress and waited until he had time to calm down, she added, "That was a long time ago."

"I don't care how long ago it was. He turned his back on our father, and he did the same thing to us. How can you be so quick to forgive?"

Emma let the air in the cab settle. "Isn't that what we're supposed to do? Besides, I'm sure he had his reasons. Won't you at least give the man a chance?"

"I'm not giving him the time of day, if you want to, I can't stop you, but I'll have no part of it."

Emma had not seen this side of her brother and paused a few seconds before responding. "*Gott* would not want you to be so angry."

"My God, your *Gott*. I didn't see hide nor hair of him when those boys were abusing me, and to think, it could have been prevented if our so-called grandfather would've cared enough to step up to the plate."

Emma sucked in a breath and slid her teeth across her bottom lip. "Daniel, I'm sorry, I had no idea."

"Water under the bridge, but there is no way I'll be letting him back into my life."

Emma turned in his direction. "Maybe if you talk to him about it, he can help you understand his side."

Daniel's hand met the dashboard, and she flinched. For a brief moment, a bolt of panic hit her when the vein at his temple started to throb. She reached for the door. "I think I'd better go."

He didn't say a word as she slid from the seat and jumped back as soon as snow sprayed her when he pulled away.

An eerie chill ran up her spine when she recalled him mentioning more of his past. A part of her believed his reaction had little to do with their grandfather and more to do with the demons haunting him. She couldn't get home fast enough to talk to Matthew.

~~

Daniel pulled into the Mini Mart at the edge of town, leaving the engine running while he went in to buy a six-pack. Two grimy teenage boys stood in line before him and his stomach churned when memories blurred between the past and the present. He couldn't escape fast enough to dull the visions in his mind.

He found himself back at Willow Creek, in the same pull-off where he left Emma. The brown paper bag perched on the seat beside him urged him to reach inside. For a split-second, he reasoned with himself about popping the first tab. As he held the can to his lips, he thought. *"I can stop whenever I want."*

He chugged the first can, rolled the window down, and threw it out before reaching for another. Soon he was numb to reality. Temporarily free from his past. After the fifth can littered the ground, he reached under the seat and pulled out a brown bottle of dark liquid. It burned his throat as he emptied it in one long gulp, soothing the pain with another malty ale.

He pressed his cheek against the cold glass and closed his eyes. *The blue room from his nightmares took over his unconsciousness. The two faces taunting him were forever etched in the darkness-one muffling his scream, the other clanging the key against the metal lock. The rag stuffed in his mouth, along with their rank odor, made him gag.*

Bile rose in his throat just as he opened his eyes. As if in slow motion, he tried to lift his head from the window. Before he knew what happened, his door opened, and his face met the frozen dirt along with the toe of a black boot. His body was numb as a heel pressed on his shoulder, forcing him to his back. A calloused hand reached out to yank him up. When his body wouldn't cooperate, two hands lifted him off the ground and propped him up against the side of the truck. His head refused to stay upright. He clung to the side view mirror, slack-jawed, and slumped over before he slipped back to the ground.

~~

Light filtered in between the slats of the yellowed blinds, forcing Daniel to crack his eyelids. The pounding behind his eyes prevented him from lifting his head, but the stench from the flea-invested room reminded him of how low he sank. After losing his job and being kicked out of his adoptive parent's house, it was the place he now called home. Sprawled out across the bed in the same clothes he wore the day before, he squinted at the digital clock. His keys, typically on the hook by the door, sat between the dimmed light and a cardboard cup on the nightstand. The aroma of coffee filled his nose, and he fought to sit up.

He wrapped his fingers around the still-warm cup and looked around the room. Everything was a blur, including how he got home. He pressed his fingers against the bridge of his nose and rubbed firmly, trying to find any recollection of the day before. It was slowly coming back. Emma. The boys at the Mini Mart. A black boot. That's where it ended, no matter how hard he tried to put the pieces together.

His legs felt heavy as he made his way to the bathroom. He braced himself at the counter and looked in the mirror. A picture of his father was tucked under the rusty mirror clip. Unsure how it got there, he remembered it from a few months earlier. His mother had spent an afternoon telling them about their biological father. She handed them each an old photo to keep. Who had tucked the tattered image into the mirror? The similarity to the picture stared back at him, and he dry heaved in the sink.

Dark shadows under his eyes and his sandy brown hair looked unfamiliar as his reflection bounced off the dirty mirror. The tattered Polaroid of his father in English clothes left a part of him wondering if history was repeating itself. A splash of cold water left him staring back at the man he'd become. He was on the verge of pushing away everyone that meant something to him. While that hadn't bothered him over the last few months, the truth of it all was starting to settle in.

Always within arm's reach, the familiar black label's raw liquid calmed the throbbing in his head. He kicked off his shoes, turned on the shower, and stepped inside, fully clothed. The hot water momentarily cleared his head long enough to let Katie Yoder in. If anyone could draw him out of this dark hole, the fresh innocent face of the young Amish girl would be the one.

He struggled to strip out of the wet clothes. Still curious as to how he made it home, he dressed and gathered his keys. A fresh layer of snow covered the windshield, and he hardly let a clear spot melt away before backing out of the parking lot. A quick stop at the Mini Mart and a call to his drinking buddies, and all would be well. Before he made plans for the evening, he drove down Mystic Mill Road and past Yoder Strawberry Acres. He had already set an internal reminder to pay a visit to the youth gathering the next day. He drove away from town with an unnerving desire to catch a glimpse of the sweet dark-haired girl.

A gentle and steady progression of a yellow-topped buggy forced him to let up on the gas. The snow-packed road made it difficult for the horse as it struggled to pull it up the slippery hill. It hadn't been the first time he'd been caught behind the slow-moving vehicle, but for some reason, he itched to pass the daily reminder of what could have been. As soon as they crested the hill, he pulled around the horse and left it but a small picture in his rear-view mirror.

Ahead, a small figure dotted the landscape at the side of the road. The white fields did little to hide flashes of purple blowing gracefully under the long black coat. Without a doubt, the young girl was precisely who he hoped to catch a glimpse of. He slowed to a stop and pressed the button to open the passenger side window.

"It's my lucky day."

Her rosy cheeks formed a smile, and she moved to the open window. "Hello, Daniel. What's got you out and about today? Are you headed to Emma's?"

"Something like that." He wouldn't be quick to admit she was the reason for his drive this far out, but if she thought he was on his way to the Byler's, so be it.

"I could ask you the same thing. Where are you going?"

"I finished my chores, so I'm on my way to Emma's. She's been out of sorts and I wanted to check on her."

"Hop in, and I'll take you there."

She scanned over her shoulder before answering. "I'm not sure that's a good idea."

"Why not?"

She hesitated before she opened the door and once again looked down the road before she agreed.

Daniel sat taller and turned up the heat. "Now, isn't this better than fighting the cold?"

"I quite enjoy a brisk walk."

"So do I, but I'll take a warm engine over frozen feet any day."

He turned off the radio as she settled in her seat. He pulled back to the center of the road toward the Byler farm. In one swift move, Katie slid down to the floorboard as soon as they reached Emma's driveway. "Oh, no!"

Alarmed at her quick attempt to get out of view, he asked, "What's the matter?"

"There's my *datt's* buggy."

"Okay, what's the problem?"

"Please, Daniel. Leave!"

The urgency in her voice left him no option but to put the truck in reverse.

Once they were far enough away from the Byler farm, Katie sat up and looked out the rear window.

Glancing in his rear-view mirror he said, "Do you want to tell me what that was all about? Does it have anything to do with your parents thinking I'm a bad influence again?"

"Something like that."

"Should I take you home?"

Katie looked out the back window one more time and folded her hands on her lap. "Quite honestly, I don't want to go home yet. Can we take a ride?"

"Sure, where do you want to go?"

"How about the Outlet Mall?"

Chapter 7

Katie's Cry

Katie sat flanked by Emma and Anna with her hands spread out on her lap as she anxiously waited for the three-hour service to end. The guilt of spending the day with Daniel the day before, left her wanting to escape the eyes of everyone she lied to. Emma thought she spent the day helping her *mamm*, and her parents assumed she spent the day with Emma. She wanted so badly to confide in her best friend. But Emma made it clear she was not all that happy with Daniel at the moment, so she kept her guilt-ridden conscience to herself.

Her hands filled with moisture as she wiped her palms on her blue dress. She mostly wore that color since Daniel told her how pretty she looked in blue. They had spent the whole afternoon walking around the Grove City Mall; he even treated her to a cinnamon pastry at the food court. Even if it wasn't as good as what she could make, the sweet treat held an unforgettable memory. At one point, he even took her hand as they weaved around a bus unloading a group of shoppers.

When someone tried to take her picture, he pulled her in tight and shielded her from the camera. His hold on her made her feel safe and protected, and she melted into his brown leather jacket. The earthy smell etched in her nose as she breathed in every ounce of his closeness. They were far from the group of tourists before he finally released his hold. When he did, he stopped and looked deeply into her eyes, and bent down to kiss her forehead. Her heart quickened at the memory of his embrace.

She looked past the minister and fixated on the clock on the wall. His words had little effect on her as she blocked his sermon from her mind and thought only of Daniel.

From everything Emma shared with her, she so wanted to tell her they were wrong about him. He was a perfect gentleman and showed no sign of being out of control. She couldn't deny she smelled a hint of beer on his breath, but nothing that made her believe he had a problem.

Emma elbowed her in the side when she didn't turn in her seat and kneel before the bench. The row of girls had already made it to their knees before she realized she was so lost in her daydream she completely missed the cue from the minister.

The bench butted up against the double window in her parents' living room, which had been transformed into a church. A line of yellow-topped buggies stood between her and the fence lining their driveway. Everyone in the room had their heads bowed, but at that moment, she couldn't take her concerns to the Lord. A glimpse of movement near the fence caught her eye. There was no doubt that the blue baseball cap belonged to the same young man she spent the last three hours fantasizing about.

Even though she couldn't see his face, there was something in the way he stood that was unnerving. If only she could invite him in and make him feel welcome. For some reason, she knew that would never happen. He was an outsider and wouldn't be welcome regardless of the connection he had with Emma. For the first time all morning, she dropped her head and prayed *Gott* would help her find a way to change her parent's mind.

~~

Daniel parked at the end of the fence and walked between the row of buggies. The bright sun hurt his eyes as the night before played havoc with his vision. Sunday morning always left him aching to belong, and ever since he spent the afternoon with Katie, there was an emptiness he couldn't seem to fill.

In Sugarcreek, he felt welcomed at their church, but here in Willow Springs, he was an outcast. Every day, the question that played in his mind since he learned of his grandfather's betrayal was, where did he belong? Was he a product of his biological father's bad choices, and why would his own grandfather leave him alone to fight the ugly world on his own? Only his nightly binges chased the questions away and made the day worth getting through.

A burst of January air moved through his cotton shirt, forcing him to leave and retreat to his truck. Not sure where he left his jacket the night before, he turned the heat up and pulled away from his hiding spot.

The drive back into town did little to clear his head as he pulled into an empty spot in front of the Mini Mart. A stale biscuit and a cup of coffee might help him make sense of the time he couldn't place from the night before. Katie's sweet voice rang in his head as he recalled how she smelled of sugar and cinnamon when he pulled her close. Her tiny frame and silky skin sent shivers down his spine as he recalled how her forehead tasted against his lips.

She was five years younger than him, and he had no right to think it would ever work between them. There was something about her he found exciting. The coffee left a bitter aftertaste in his mouth, much like the aftermath of learning his roots belonged deep in Holmes County. The greasy ham and cheese biscuit left a circle on the paper napkin as he stirred cream into the dark liquid. The sight of it made his stomach churn, and he threw it in the trash as he headed out the door.

The steam from the cup warmed his hand as he climbed back inside his truck. Folded neatly on the seat were his jacket and a white envelope with his name printed across the front. An eerier mass settled between his eyes and he looked in his rear-view mirror and over the dashboard. Practically dropping the cup in the holder, he reached for the note and held it close to examine it. Void of any other markings, he slid his finger along the seal and pulled a simple piece of paper from its envelope. A few simple words were all it held.

> *Daniel,*
> *You'll never find what you're looking for in an empty bottle. This is not the path God planned for you.*
> *"Be not quick in your spirit to become angry, for anger lodges in the heart of fools."*
> *Ecclesiastes 7:9*
> *JS*

He turned the simple lined paper over, hoping it held another clue. Nothing but a blank page, so he concentrated on the signature again. Who did he know with those initials? When no one came to mind, he tossed the envelope on the dashboard and mumbled. *"Just what I need. Another secret to unravel."*

~~

With the blinds turned down, he hung the keys on the hook and threw himself across the unmade bed. The stench from the sour clothes on the floor filled the room, and he pulled a pillow over his face. If he timed it right, he could sleep through the afternoon and still make it to the youth gathering that evening. He already planned to park where he couldn't be seen and quietly find a way to lure Katie away from the activity.

As he drifted between reality and deep sleep, the haunting blue walls came into view. Two figures towered over him as he huddled in the corner. The door's lock broke free, and light from the hallway engulfed a gray haired gentleman who called his name. When he lifted his face to meet the stranger's eyes, the alarm on his phone woke him from the past.

He opened his eyes, the day had turned into night, and the streetlight was the only thing that lit the room through the cracks in the window coverings. A wave of peace filled the room as the lingering image of his adoptive father came to mind. Without hesitating, he reached for his phone and tapped on his father's face.

It only rang twice before his father's voice echoed on the other end. "Daniel."

Without letting him continue with his greeting, he stuttered. "The night ...nightmares are back. Whatever happened to them?"

"Daniel, we've talked about this before. They were troubled boys."

Raising his voice, he replied, "But dad, do you understand what they did to me? I can never forgive them."

His father said in a hushed tone, "I do."

"Does all of this have anything to do with your poor choices lately?"

Silence filled the line as Daniel tried to come to terms with his father's question. When he didn't respond, his father continued.

"Son, you need to understand we each have our own path in life. You can choose to follow the path of righteousness or choose the route that leads you to destruction. I don't believe the one you're on is what God has planned for you."

Daniel snapped at his father's words. "What did you say?"

"God's path? I don't believe this is the course He had in mind."

"That's the second time I've heard that today."

"Well, I guess He wants to make a point to you then. You need to find a way to forgive the wrongs of your past and move on."

"I've got to go." Before his father had a chance to press him more, he disconnected the call.

He tossed the phone on the bed, propped his elbows on his knees and rested his head in his hands, and thought. *I've given Him plenty of chances to direct my way, and what good did it do me? The bottle in the drawer will do the trick faster than God.*

~~

The afternoon dragged on as Katie anticipated the evening *singeon*. She'd seen to the snacks, and Samuel and *Datt* lined up benches in the enclosed building. Kerosene heaters were warming it nicely, and she laid out songbooks on the table separating the benches. Girls on one side, boys on the other, only to exchange an occasional glance between them. No matter how badly she wanted Daniel to attend, she knew she shouldn't encourage it ...if only she could find a way to be with him again. A mixture of shame and excitement clouded her judgment as she tried to make sense of her feelings.

The door opened, and Emma came in, pulling her away from her longing thoughts.

"I decided to walk over early in case you needed help with anything."

"I think we have everything under control, and I suspect the youth will start showing up anytime now."

Emma removed her brown bonnet and held her hands over one of the heaters to warm her fingertips. "It's a shame the ice on the pond isn't thick enough yet. It would've been nice to spend the afternoon skating."

Katie patted the seat next to her. "I bet in a couple of weeks; it will be perfect. Samuel said he'd check it next week to see how it was coming."

With the mention of Samuel's name, Emma's face turned cold as she asked. "Are you going to tell me what happened between the two of you? He's been in a foul mood for weeks now."

"I suppose I have a bit to do with his attitude."

"I figured as much. Do you want to talk about it?"

Emma ran her fingers over the edge of the Hymnal and took her time answering. "He wants more than I can promise."

"What's that supposed to mean? You and Samuel are meant to be together."

"I'm only sixteen. I don't know what I want to do next week, let alone commit to marrying someone in two years."

"I can't imagine Samuel rushing you. He's always known there was an age difference between the two of you. Besides, he's waited this long, what's another two years?"

"I can't expect him to wait for me."

"Don't you think that's up to him?"

"I suppose, but I'm too young to be thinking about marriage."

Katie twisted the ribbon from her *kapp*. "I don't think sixteen is too young to marry."

"What? Do you really think you're ready to commit to something so serious at this age?"

Katie lowered her voice. "If the right person came along, I don't think age would matter. When you fall in love, you just know it."

"You're trying to tell me something. Spill it!"

A sly smile crossed Katie's lips. "I can't imagine what you're talking about."

"Who is he?"

Katie swung her legs over the bench and headed to the snack table, avoiding the prying eyes of her best friend as she said over her shoulder, "He's not from this *g'may.*"

Emma was about to ask another question, but a group of girls walked through the door, giving Katie the perfect out to another lie.

~~

Emma enjoyed the fellowship while the group sang some of their favorite hymns. After the last song, the girls gathered in small groups, hoping someone special would lure them away. Some of the boys went outside, and some lingered, waiting for the perfect time to ask someone special if they could give them a ride home. One by one, couples disappeared into the night.

From across the room, Emma noticed Samuel talking to Edna Graber. Her heart skipped a beat as Edna held on to his every word. He smiled and tried to seem interested when all along she knew he had one ear to Edna and one eye keyed in on her. Had she made a mistake by cutting things off with him? The room suddenly felt warm. She reached for her coat and bonnet and headed to the door. Once outside, she leaned on the door and lightly bounced her head off the metal and thought. *I know I did the right thing; how can I ask him to wait for something I'm not sure will ever happen?*

The door behind her moved, and she stumbled as it opened. Before falling face first in the snow, Samuel wrapped his arm around her middle and pulled her upright. He mouthed in her ear. "Can we talk?"

"About?"

"What do you think? About what you're doing to us, of course."

"I don't think there's any point."

Samuel took her hand and pulled her to the side of the building. He gently pushed her back up to the wall and rested his hands on either side of her shoulders.

She hung her head until he lifted her chin with one finger. "Look at me."

The moon threw shadows on his face when she tried to see the line of his jaw in the dark. He brushed the back of his hand on her cheek. "Please don't do this to us. I promise I'll be patient and not push." He lowered his hand to her chest and tapped lightly. "I know somewhere deep inside of here you know I'll love no one else, and I find it hard to believe you don't feel the same way."

He moved his hands to her shoulders. "I dare you to deny you don't feel the same." In one precious moment... and one she'd remember for the rest of her life; he molded his lips over hers. When she didn't respond, he moved his face ever so slightly and pleaded.

"At least give me this one last memory. If it's all I get, I'll treasure it forever."

No matter how hard she wanted to deny his request, she yearned to feel the love he had for her. She raised her hand to his dimpled chin and pulled him in close. Losing herself in the softness of his touch, she let him caress her lips with his own for a few seconds before she ducked under his arm and ran home.

~~

Katie slipped outside as quickly as her friend's attention turned to the boys in the room. The clear sky made a perfect backdrop for the bright moon that guided her way to the backside of the barn. From where she stood, hidden behind the cover of the strawberry shed, she watched headlights as they filtered through the trees. If Daniel pulled off to the side of the road, she'd see his lights from her hiding spot.

Thankfully, she remembered to hide a pair of long tights in a bucket behind the barn, she pulled them up under her skirt for extra warmth. In the distance, she heard the clip-clop of buggies leaving, all headed in different directions away from the farm.

From out of nowhere, Daniel's arm circled her middle. He let out a slight moan in her ear and nibbled at her neck, moving his hand up her waist in an inappropriate manner. "Waiting for someone special?" he asked in a husky rattle.

The stench of his breath attacked her senses, and she pulled from his grip. "You startled me, and you've been drinking."

"It looked like you were waiting for someone. Could that be me?"

He pulled her closer, turned her around, and rested his hands on her hips. "I even saw you pull pants on under your dress. A bold thing to do out in the open, even for an Amish girl. I thought you were supposed to be all prim and proper."

She took a step back, trying to put space between them, but he held tighter. "It was cold, and I didn't know how long I might have to wait. Were you watching me? Why didn't you let me know you were here?"

With a slight slur of his words and a pat to her bottom, he said seductively, "I was enjoying the show."

"You've been drinking. I should go."

"Go? But I just got here. I thought we could go for a ride."

"I don't think you're in any shape to drive."

He stumbled backward and caught himself on a tree. "I put my ol' girl in drive, and she takes me where I want to go." He reached up and touched her cheek. "Tonight, I want to see more of this pretty face."

Her stomach flipped when he tried to draw her closer. He lost his footing and fell to the ground, landing her on top of him. "Now, just where I want you." He reached up and pulled the back of her head toward his face, letting his lips freely explore her mouth.

He tasted vile, and she struggled to get away from his grip. "You need to go. If my *datt* catches you here like this, we'll both be in big trouble."

She rolled off him, and they both stood. A surge of defense anchored in his voice, and he shook his fist at her. "I'm not afraid of your old man."

He teetered over, and she positioned her small frame under his shoulder and steadied him. "You might not be afraid of him, but I am." She wrapped her arm around his middle and guided him to the road. "Where did you park?"

Daniel pointed his arm to the clearing hidden behind the trees. "I knew you'd see it my way."

"I'm not going anywhere with you like this." She struggled to keep him upright, and her shoulder burned from his weight. The few minutes it took to make it to the clearing seemed like an hour as he continued to plummet her with rude comments. The words coming from his mouth were like none she had ever known. In his right mind she couldn't imagine him ever being so crude. She opened the passenger door and pushed his weight toward the seat.

"Where's your phone? I should call someone."

He grabbed her arm and pulled her inside. "Nope, don't need nobody but you."

"What's gotten into you? You're scaring me, and you need to STOP!"

His grasp on her wrist stung as he added pressure to his hold. The more she tried to jerk away, the harder he twisted. He grabbed the back of her bonnet, and it fell to the floor. When she jerked away, he grabbed her *kapp* and yanked it from her head. The pins popped out, and the hair leaving her scalp made her yelp.

"Daniel, you're hurting me," she cried.

"Ah, come on, Katie girl, let me see that hair of yours. Is it true only a husband gets to see those long locks? This guy, for one, would love to run his hands through it."

In one swift move, he pulled her inside the cab until she was on his lap. "Right where I want you. I could get used to this, but you need to stop fighting me."

Her heart raced as she pushed back by placing both hands on his chest. In one last-ditch effort, he reached for her again, and she sunk her teeth into his hand. He swung to slap her but missed and fell back, hitting his head on the steering wheel.

Without giving him another chance, she slid from his lap to the ground, catching her knee on the door frame as she fell. Unless he drove, he wouldn't be able to catch her in his condition, so she ran faster than she had ever run before. Her knee throbbed, and it wasn't until she got a safe enough distance away did she stop. Warmth pooled beneath the layers of her stockings and tights, and when she added pressure to the spot, her stomach heaved, expelling her shame.

Katie stood in the shadows of the front porch, trying to decide how she could get to her room without stopping to talk to her parents. The light from the kitchen glowed, forcing her to retreat to the strawberry stand. A desperate need to compose herself forced her to find shelter in the now darkened room. Once inside, she backed up to the wall and slid to the floor, burying her head in her hands. Tears washed her face as she pushed his betrayal from her mind. What was she thinking? Maybe her *datt* was right; he wasn't to be trusted. That's what her head told her anyway, but her heart told another story. She had to find a way to help him, and for a split second, she wondered if she had led him on. Maybe this was her fault, and she could have prevented it if she hadn't encouraged their relationship.

~~

The roar of the diesel engine rang in his ears, but Daniel couldn't lift his head from the back of the seat for the life of him. He felt his body slump toward the driver, but a strong arm pushed him to the opposite side of the seat, bouncing his head off the passenger side window. The cold pane did little to clear his head, and he gave into his stupor.

The next thing he knew, he was sitting in a bathtub with a steady stream of water showering down on him. The shock of it all brought him out of his state long enough to crawl over the side of the tub and pass out on the bathroom floor.

A long and steady beep from his phone rang like a bugle against his head. He pulled himself to a sitting position, leaning back on the door. From across the room, positioned on his bed, was a brown bonnet and a white envelope. Katie's face flashed before him, and he edged to the bed. He took the solid material, brought it to his nose, picked up the envelope, and pulled a creased sheet of paper from its confines.

Daniel,

You should be ashamed of yourself. This is not the path He sees for you.

"Let the wicked forsake his way, and the unrighteous man his thoughts; let him return to the Lord, that he may have compassion on him, and to our God, for he will abundantly pardon." Isaiah 55:7

JS

He closed his eyes and tried to remember. Who brought him home and what had he done he should be ashamed of? All of a sudden, Katie's face came to mind, and the bile in his stomach surfaced.

Chapter 8

Shame

Katie rolled over in bed and tucked her arm under her head. A sharp pain forced her eyes open. A deeply etched bruise appeared overnight, leaving four clearly outlined fingerprints across her wrist. Her *mamm's* voice from the hallway compelled her arm back under the blankets as the door opened.

"Rise and shine, sleepyhead. We have fifteen loaves of bread to make for the Sandwich Shoppe this morning."

Katie yawned. "I'm sorry I slept in, not sure what my problem is this morning. Give me a few minutes, and I'll be right down."

With a questioning look, her *mamm* asked, "Could it be you spent a late evening riding the back roads with someone special?"

Katie saw her eyes sparkle in anticipation of her answer and teased her back. "Now, wouldn't you like to know?"

Ruth snickered. "I would, but I'll not ask, and I don't expect you to tell me just yet."

The door closed before Katie allowed herself to pull her arm out and examine it closely. How was she ever going to explain it to her parents? Praying it wasn't broken and just bruised, she struggled twisting her hair up under her *kapp* and even more so pinning her dress closed. Any other day she'd roll her sleeves up to her elbows, but this time she pinned the cuffs of her dress securely around her wrists. The gash on her knee was easier to conceal beneath her winter stockings. To hide the remnants of Daniel's strength, she tucked her arms in a sweater.

The smells radiating from the kitchen pulled her downstairs in time to meet a stack of pancakes and a platter of bacon waiting on the table.

"Go ring the bell to let your *bruder* and *datt* know breakfast is ready," her *mamm* instructed as she walked through the doorway.

The brisk morning air stung her lungs as she walked to the end of the porch to ring the dinner bell. Two quick pulls on the chain and her *bruder* appeared around the side of the *haus*.

He carried an armload of kindling on the porch. "Here, take this inside; I need to go get something from the barn." He dumped the slivers of wood in her arms. She flinched and moaned, then turned away to bite her bottom lip.

"You okay?" he asked.

"Jah."

She leaned up against the porch railing and repositioned the stack in her arms before opening the door.

Mamm met her at the door. "Oh good! I was hoping Samuel would cut more. We have a lot of baking to do today."

Katie dropped the thin pieces of wood in the basket near the stove and sat at the table. Ruth laid the back of her hand across her forehead. "You look pale this morning. Are you feeling under the weather?"

Without letting her answer, she continued. "You don't feel warm. Maybe you stayed out too late, *jah*?

"I'm fine. You worry too much."

"Could be, but that's what I do. How about you fix a cup of tea. Maybe that will bring some color back to your cheeks."

Katie sorted through the tea bags in the basket on the table, found her favorite lemon balm flavor and carried it to the stove. The white porcelain teapot was filled and ready to use. With her back to her *mamm*, she struggled to pour the hot water in the cup with her left hand. How was she ever going to knead bread dough with one hand? She carried the cup to the table and added a spoonful of honey to the hot liquid and tried to find a way out of making bread.

Once everyone made it to the breakfast table, Katie bowed her head and prayed along with her family. However, her silent prayer was a plea to *Gott* to forgive her for the lie she was about to tell.

Samuel passed the plate of pancakes, and it slipped from her hands, crashing to the floor.

Ruth jumped from her chair, "For heaven's sake, child, what's gotten into you this morning?"

"I'm sorry. I tripped and fell last night and landed on my wrist. It's giving me some trouble this morning."

"You could have told us before you sent our breakfast across the floor." *Mamm* snarled. "Let me look at it."

"No need. I can move it, so it's not broken. It must be sprained."

Katie knelt on the floor to pick up the broken platter and pancakes while Samuel plucked bacon off his plate. "That's what you get for sneaking off and waking me when you came in so late."

Samuel's comment sent a flash of panic to her chest. She looked over her shoulder, but his expression was void of any clue, her heart calmed, and she continued to clean up the mess.

Ruth headed back to the stove. "Drink your coffee and give me a few minutes, and I'll make more batter."

Katie piped in. "Let me do it."

"Some help you'll be when you can't even pick up your cup without wincing. Go sit, I'll do it."

Katie settled back into her spot, picked up her tea, and took a soothing sip of its calming flavor.

Her *datt* stirred fresh cream into his coffee and asked, "Do I need to take you into town to get it looked at?"

Fear at the thought of anyone seeing the purple bruises forming on her wrist, she quickly responded, "No, really, it's fine." She held out her arm and moved her wrist around in circles, clenching her jaw. "I'm sure it's sprained." Her stomach wrenched as she forced movement to prove her point.

Her *mamm* added a few new pieces of kindling to the stove and waited for the griddle to heat back up. "So much for you helping with bread. You can take the wagon to the dry goods store and pick-up supplies instead."

A wave of relief flooded her. If she were going to make sense of anything, a brisk walk to clear her head would ease her guilt.

~~

The frozen ground made it easy to drag the green wagon along the side of the road, as she thought how the overcast sky matched her mood. A swallow, perched on top of the Byler Furniture sign, fluttered in front of her at the end of Emma's driveway. She wanted to make a detour and find comfort in her friend's embrace, but how could she ever explain Daniel's behavior? She didn't want to cloud the image of Emma's brother any more than it had been. For now, it was best she kept the whole incident to herself.

The long walk to Shetler's Dry Goods Store gave her enough time to have a talk with *Gott* and try to make sense of all that happened the night before. How could she have feelings for someone who would treat her so harshly? If that's what alcohol did to a person, she never wanted to have the tiniest taste.

After checking off everything from her list, she headed back outside. Big snowflakes started to cover the ground as she loaded the wagon. If she didn't hurry, she'd never be able to maneuver the heavy load through the mounting flurries.

If Edna Graber had not stopped her inside, she'd be halfway home by now. The young girl, obviously more interested in asking about Samuel, carried on for fifteen minutes. When Katie found a break in the conversation, she excused herself.

Thinking back to their brief exchange, a small ache seeped in at how she asked about her *bruder*. It wasn't supposed to be like this. It should be Emma asking about Samuel, not Edna.

The rumble of an engine slowing down behind her forced her to glance over her shoulder without stopping. When the familiar black vehicle came to a stop and she heard the door slam shut, she struggled to walk faster, pulling the wagon with her left hand.

"Katie, wait. Let me help."

Under her breath, she sighed through gritted teeth. "*Why, Gott? Please, I can't face him right now.*"

"I don't need your help," she answered and continued to battle the heavy cart.

He reached for her, and she jumped back. "No!"

He dropped his hand as she put distance between them.

Daniel took the handle from her hand, and she flinched, shielding her face.

He furrowed his eyebrows. "What's the matter with you? I just want to help you with this. You're never going to pull this all the way home."

Before she knew what happened, he lifted the full cart into the back of his truck, opened the passenger side door, and pointed for her to get inside.

Fear froze her to the ground at the side of the road. There was no way she was getting in. That was until a softness in his eyes spoke to her.

"Come on. I promise I'll take you straight home and even drop you off at the end of the driveway."

Without saying a word, she climbed inside and kept one hand on the door handle. If he made one move toward her, she'd jump out with no regard to her safety. He made his way inside, glaring at her in a questioning manner. There was a heaviness between them as he sat with both hands gripped to the steering wheel. He drew in a deep breath. "I don't remember much about last night, but bits and pieces. Do you know how I got home?"

How could he not remember? She thought. Her wrist throbbed, and her knee ached with the recollection. "Just take me home."

She continued to look straight ahead. "Katie, please look at me. Tell me what happened last night."

There was a plea in his voice that touched her somewhere deep inside. "You really don't remember?"

It took him a few seconds to respond. "I had too much to drink, and sometimes I don't remember things -- like who I talked to or how I get home. I wanted to see you, that's about all I remember. From there, things are a blur."

She pulled herself closer to the door. "Why?"

He reached for her, and she cringed, hoping his outstretched hand wouldn't meet hers. "Why what?" he asked.

"Why are you drinking so much?"

"I'm not sure. I guess it's a way to forget. Why do you ask?"

She hesitated and wondered how much she should say. The Daniel before her was nothing like the one from last night, but she still was apprehensive about his reaction to her questions. "You change when you've been drinking, and I'm trying to understand. What's so bad you have to drown it away?"

He moved his hand back to the steering wheel, and his voice cracked when he responded. "Things I want to forget."

She waited to see if he would say anything else and when she was sure he was through, she said, "I know I'm not very old, and I don't know about things like this but isn't there someone you can talk to. Maybe your dad or a minister?"

He tapped his thumb on the steering wheel. "How much has Emma shared with you about our past?"

"A little. I know your mom and dad were from Sugarcreek."

"Did you know our dad was Amish?"

She shifted slightly. "No, I didn't."

"I might have an Amish background, but it's not something I'm proud of."

In a murmur, she asked, "But why?"

The gentleness in his voice disappeared. "It's a long story and one I'd rather not get into right now."

He pulled back out on the road, and they rode in silence for the next ten minutes. When they got within minutes from her house, she said, "Stop here. I'll walk the rest of the way."

The back end fishtailed as he braked. "Are you going to tell me why the silent treatment? Does this have anything to do with your father? He barely knows me and all of a sudden, I'm not respectable enough."

"You have it all wrong."

"How about you explain it to me because, in my books, I'll never be good enough for your kind."

Katie pulled back on her mittens. "Getting close to me isn't the issue, it's probably the drinking he's concerned about. According to him, you're trouble. He called it abusive behavior that he won't tolerate."

"Abusive behavior, what's that supposed to mean? When do a few beers and a bottle of Jack constitute abusive behavior?"

She waited for him to stop before she opened the door and met him at the back of the truck.

He brushed the snow from the wagon before lifting it to the ground. "Your *datt* is no different from my grandfather."

"Your grandfather?"

"Yep, the one and only Bishop Shetler."

"The bishop that came to Stella's funeral from Sugarcreek?" She asked.

"Yep, he's the one. The one who didn't have enough family loyalty to claim me as his own because of his pride."

Katie reached for the handle and pulled the wagon to the side of the road. "I'm sorry you have to deal with all of that, but I believe there has to be a better way than drinking."

Smugly, he hollered as she walked away. "You tell me one good reason why my drinking is anyone's business but my own."

She stopped in her tracks, dropped the handle of the wagon, and turned to face him. "I'll tell you four."

She yanked her mitten off and pushed her coat sleeve up, revealing four distinctive finger marks as a fresh set of tears rolled down her cheeks.

Before he responded, she turned and dragged the cart through the snow and back down the road toward home.

~~

The shock of seeing the bruises left him speechless as he watched her walk away. As if in slow motion, slivers of the scene from the night before played over in his head. There was no doubt by the look in her eyes he had been the one responsible. What had he done, and how could he lose so much of himself he didn't realize he hurt her? Bile lodged in the back of his throat, and he dropped to his knees.

~~

Winded, Katie pulled the cart to the back porch and leaned on the railing. The back door swung open, and Emma stood resting her hands on her hips.

"There you are. Your *mamm* and I were just getting ready to send your *datt* out to look for you."

"No need for that. It was a little challenging pulling the wagon through the snow, but I made it." Katie responded.

Emma helped her carry in the baking supplies and sat at the table as she took off her coat and bonnet. "I must have just missed you this morning. You should have stopped by, and I would have gone with you."

A twinge of shame lingered on Katie's shoulders while she put groceries away, hoping her tardiness wouldn't be questioned. "I ran into Edna Graber this morning. She sure does like to talk. I had a hard time bowing out of the conversation without being rude."

Katie tried to ignore the flinch Emma made at the mention of Edna's name. "I don't think she was too interested in talking to me as much as she wanted to ask what Samuel was up to."

Emma stirred an empty spoon in her cup of tea. "I saw him talking to her last night. Do you think he drove her home?"

Katie stopped and turned toward Emma's pining tone. "Does that bother you?"

"It shouldn't, but I guess if I was honest, it does."

Katie pulled a chair out and sat beside her. "Are you sure this is what you want? I'm certain Samuel only paid attention to her to make you jealous."

Emma took a sip of tea before adding. "I don't have any right since I'm not ready to give him what he wants."

Katie rested her elbow on the table and nestled her chin in her palm. "You know, growing up isn't all it's cracked up to be. Somedays I wish we were kids again with nothing to worry about but playing in the creek and sneaking fresh strawberries from the fields."

A small giggle escaped Emma's lips before she replied. "Now, isn't that the truth?"

Emma laid her hand on Katie's arm, and she grimaced. Katie turned away, her sweater's sleeve moved up, and Emma's eyes caught the darkened color and gasped. "Katie!"

Katie looked over her shoulder, hoping her *mamm* was still in the basement. "Shh..."

Emma tilted in and gingerly pushed up the wool on her arm. "Katie, this isn't a fall like your *mamm* spoke of."

She pulled Emma to her feet and dragged her toward the stairs. They didn't stop until they were safely behind her bedroom door.

Both girls sat on Katie's bed. "Who did this to you?"

Tears spilled over her bottom lashes. "Daniel."

Chapter 9

Forgiven

The streetlight flickered above Daniel's head as he sat on the stone steps of the Presbyterian Church. All afternoon he'd driven on every back road in Willow Springs, circling past the Yoder farm more than once. It took all he had not to pull in and beg for Katie's forgiveness. The marks, his marks, left on her ivory skin bore a hole in his heart.

Drawn to the two-hundred-year-old structure at the edge of town, he hoped to find comfort in God's house. When the double red doors did little to allow him in, he sat on the top step and buried his head in his hands. *If only I could talk to her*, he thought. *Maybe she'll forgive me. Oh, God! What have I done? Lord, this is not who I am. Please, Lord, help me.*

The sky turned black as the cold cement penetrated his jeans. The familiar clip-clop of an approaching buggy caught his attention as he followed the sound. At every turn, he was reminded of his past. A heritage that bound him to an existence he felt detached from. *What is it? What are you trying to show me?*

A gust of wind blew around the building, yet a warm breeze settled on his face. From somewhere deep inside, he heard. *Which path will you choose?* He looked to the sky and hollered. *What choice do I have?*

"It all depends on which one will glorify Him," a voice said behind him.

An older gentleman stood in the doorway, and heat spilled outside. "Would you like to come in?"

He turned in the man's direction and stood. Simultaneously, visions of Emma, Marie, Melvin, and Katie flashed before his eyes. Lurking in the dark were the boys from his childhood and his biological father's drunken rages. Good and bad mixed together in a kaleidoscope of memories.

A movement outside caught his eye, but it disappeared as quickly as the man who'd invited him inside. The door shut, the light illuminating the stained-glass behind the pulpit tugged at him. He walked toward the pew where he usually sat, listening to God's word with his adoptive parents. It had been months since he'd been in the sanctuary, and he inched closer toward the light, never taking his eyes off the image etched in the glass. The closer he got, the stronger the urge to drop to his knees became. When he stopped at the familiar pew, he rested his hand on the polished wood and mouthed ...*Please forgive me.*

Before he gave God time to reach him, he ran from the building and didn't stop until he made it back to his truck. Tucked up under the windshield was a white envelope. The message inside released a fresh surge of regret.

Daniel,

Jeremiah 32:18 says the consequences of sin from one generation are visited on the next. Each generation has the choice to stop the cycle. You do have a choice, don't let history repeat itself. This is not the path God has for you.

JS

Who was this person, and how did he know? It had to be the shadow he saw before entering the church. He turned the key and waited for the cold interior to warm a spot on the cold glass. As he pulled back out in the street, he saw the outline of a man. His black hat and dark clothes blended into the night, barely making him visible. It only took a second to look in the rearview mirror and back at the silhouette to find the image gone. Had he indeed saw something or was he imagining it?

Instead of turning in the dirty hotel's parking lot, he followed his heart and pulled up in front of his parent's house. The wreath on the front door, leftover from Christmas, welcomed him home. Suddenly, the urge to drown his pain was replaced by an overwhelming need to make it right with his parents. He bowed his head and pleaded with God to help him find the words. When he opened his eyes, both of his parents stood on the porch.

The walk up the steps and into his dad's waiting arms seemed to take an eternity. With each step, months of despair shed from his shoulders. When he finally got close enough to accept the embrace of the one man who loved him unconditionally, he cried out. "I've done something horrible."

His father pulled him close. "Son, I'm sure whatever you've done can be forgiven."

"Can I forgive myself?"

"Come inside and tell us. I'm sure between the three of us, we will find a solution."

He let his father lead him through the door and slipped his boots off on the mat.

His mother reached up and kissed his cheek. "Go into the study with your father, and I'll fix you something warm to drink. Have you eaten?"

"I couldn't eat even if I wanted to."

"It looks like you haven't eaten in weeks." She laid her hand on his cheek. "You need to come home."

"I do," was all he said as he followed his father into the study.

He walked to the fire and held his hands out over the roaring heat from the stone fireplace. With his back to his father, he took in a deep breath before turning toward him. "I hurt someone I care about."

His father sat in one of the two brown leather chairs that faced the hearth and pointed to the one to his left. "Sit."

Daniel made his way to his father's side.

"Now, how about you start from the beginning?"

"I don't even know where to start because I don't remember most of it. All I know is what I saw."

"What's that?"

"Bruises."

He waited for the look on his father's face to change to disgust, much like how he felt every time the vision of Katie's wrist came to mind, but it didn't.

"Bruises on who?"

"Katie Yoder."

"Levi and Ruth's, Katie?"

In a stern but loving manner, his father said. "Explain."

"I don't remember much other than the cry in her voice. I went to see her at the youth gathering Sunday night. I remember being out with a few friends beforehand, but I don't remember driving there or even how I got home."

"How can you be sure the bruises came from you?" His father asked.

"It was as clear as the fear on her face I was to blame, but I don't remember what I did or why I used so much force that I left marks."

His father propped his elbows on the arms of his chair and rested his chin on his folded knuckles.

"I'm not going to say I'm not disappointed in your behavior but admitting you're at fault is half the battle."

91

The flames held Daniel's gaze as he squeezed the arms of the chair. "How am I ever going to make this right?"

"You need to make it right with God first."

"I'm not too sure He's happy with me right now."

"God always forgives. The issue is most people can't forgive themselves, and they blame Him for their own actions. We all have free will, and it's up to each one of us to choose the path we follow."

Daniel snapped. "I keep hearing that."

His father pointed to the framed print above the fireplace. "Read that."

Daniel read the words. *"Trust in the Lord with all your heart and lean not on your own understanding; in all your ways submit to Him, and He will make your paths straight." - Proverbs 3:5-6*

He whispered. "I can't see God in my life?"

His father waited a few moments before answering. "Not right now because you've pushed Him out, but He's always there."

Daniel walked to the window and stared into the night.

His father's voice echoed off the ten-foot ceiling. "It doesn't matter what you've done. Even the things you think are unforgivable. God says He will make it right if you submit and follow Him. No matter where you are on your journey, you can choose to turn around and follow, allowing Him to lead you on the right path."

Daniel returned to his seat. "I'm angry at Melvin."

"Then it's time you face him."

"It makes me sick thinking about it."

His father stood to add a log to the fire and pointed to the picture. "See that word. It says *paths*, not a path. There are many paths we can choose to take. You can spend a lifetime holding a grudge against your grandfather or drinking yourself into a stupor you don't remember. But at the end of the day, it's your choice."

Daniel dropped his head. "I've not been making the best choices lately."

"No, you haven't, but you need to realize that. No one can do that for you. Maybe the Lord put Katie in your path to show you what forgiveness looks like."

He buried his head in his hands. "How can she ever forgive me?"

"Have you asked?"

"No."

His mother walked through the door carrying a tray. After setting it down, she rested her hand on his shoulder and pulled him close and whispered in a loving tone. "God calms the storm, but sometimes God rages the storm to calm His child."

Emma paced between her bedroom windows, watching the driveway, praying Matthew would come home. She never felt so much rage toward another person, and she wouldn't rest until she talked to her *bruder*. Daniel was out of control, and if anyone was going to get through to him, it would be Matthew. She dug out the cell phone Daniel had given her and tucked it in her pocket. If Matthew wouldn't agree to help, she'd take matters into her own hands. When the minutes turned into an hour, she walked downstairs and made a cup of tea, hoping it would calm her nerves.

The porcelain kettle on the back of the stove stayed warm, and she poured hot water over a waiting tea bag. Her *datt* sat at the table reading a paper as she moved to the window and then back to the table.

"What's got you so anxious?" He asked.

"I need to talk to Matthew. Do you know when he'll be back?"

"Tomorrow afternoon."

"Tomorrow! But I need to talk to him tonight."

He folded his paper in half and laid it on the table. "Anything I can help with?"

Emma pulled a chair out beside him. "No, not this time."

"There used to be a day when your old *datt* could fix anything. Are you too big for that now?"

The softness in his voice tugged at her heart, making her smile. "I'm never too big for your help, but this time I think Matthew is better suited for the job."

"How about you give me a try."

Emma stirred a spoon of honey in her cup and wondered how he'd react to what worried her.

"It's Daniel"

"What about Daniel?"

"He's not been himself, and I don't know what to do about it."

"Not so sure you can do anything about it. Sometimes people need to work through things in their own mind, and no amount of worry from those they love can fix it."

She let the clock on the wall finish its chime before continuing. "He's hurting those around him, and he can't see it."

"Does this have anything to do with his drinking?"

"How do you know about that?"

"Levi stopped by the other day to warn me."

"Warn you about what?"

"About him spending too much time with you and Matthew."

A cold chill ran up the back of Emma's neck with the thought of Levi finding out what Daniel had done to Katie. What would her own *datt* do if something like that happened to her? She repositioned herself in her chair and taking a slow sip of her tea asked, "Why does he think we need to stay clear of him?"

Jacob snapped the paper back open. "Seems the boy's been raising Cain all over town. He lost his job and even got himself kicked out of his father's house. Up to no good by the looks of it."

In not much more than a whisper, she replied, "More than you know."

Jacob dropped the paper and peered over the black and white print. "What was that?"

Emma carried her cup to the sink. "Nothing, it's not important."

"I think Levi has a point. Maybe you and Matthew need to stay clear of him until he gets his act together."

She didn't answer but reached for her coat and bonnet hanging by the back door. "I think I'll go for a walk."

Her *datt* looked over the rim of his glasses, perched low on his nose, and said, "The temperature's dropping, so don't stay out too long."

Emma stood on the back porch, wrapped her blue scarf around her neck, and headed to the feed shed, patting the phone in her pocket through the layer of wool. She needed to talk to Daniel without waiting for Matthew; it couldn't wait a minute longer.

A puff of snow circled around her feet as she pushed open the door. The bins of feed welcomed her into the small cinderblock building. She found the flashlight near the door and located an overturned bucket to use as a chair. Her chilled fingertips struggled to retrieve the phone, and it took her a moment to find the power button. Thank goodness Daniel insisted she charge it when she saw him last. Before she tapped his picture on the screen, she changed her mind and clicked on Nathan Bouteright's number instead.

The phone only rang twice before the voice on the other end answered. "Bouteright's Stables."

"Nathan?"

"Yes, this is Nathan Bouteright. May I help you?"

"It's Emma ...Emma Byler."

"Emma, what a nice surprise. Are you looking for your mother?"

"Actually, I was eager to talk to you."

"Is everything okay?"

"Not really, it's Daniel. He's out of control, and I'm worried about him. He's been drinking too much, and I just found out he hurt one of my friends."

"Hurt how? Did he start a fight with someone?"

"Worse than that, he left bruises on my friend Katie's arm."

A few seconds of silence passed before she continued. "Nathan, I'm worried, and I don't know what to do. He's been making a name for himself all over town and not a proper one at that. He's always looked up to you. I was hoping you could talk to him. Maybe he'll listen to you."

"Emma, Daniel has demons from his past, and it may take more than a call from me to get through to him. I thought he'd worked through most of them years ago, but I think they found their way back to the surface when he found out about his family."

Emma asked, "I thought his drinking was because of Melvin. Do you think it's more than that?"

"I do, but I won't go into details since it's not my story to tell. But he's dealing with more than Melvin's refusal to own up to his responsibility."

"Nathan, please tell me what to do. My *datt* doesn't want me to reach out to him, and the community is pegging him as bad news. I can't turn my back on him; he's my *bruder*."

"What he needs is some old fashion hard work. I could use some help at the stables. If we can get him to come back to Sugarcreek, that might be a place to start."

Emma paused and then eagerly said, "I think I can help. I want to come back and visit. If I can get him to bring me, you could convince him to stay."

"Now Emma, that would be going against your *datt's* wishes. You can't let Daniel's problems come between you and your family."

"I'm on my *Rumspringa,* and I don't think he'll keep me from visiting Marie. He might not like it, but I don't think he'll stop me."

"Your *datt's* been through enough; how about you let me hire a driver to bring you over."

"I appreciate it, Nathan, but I want Daniel to drive me. It makes more sense."

"Okay, if you're sure. I'll tell Marie we should expect you sometime soon then?"

"Yes, please do. Is it okay if we show up without any notice?"

"My *haus* is always open to the both of you," he answered.

His warm welcome warmed Emma's heart. "Thank you. We'll see you soon."

"Take care, Emma."

She held the power button down, and the phone went dark. The flashlight started to dim as she made her way back to the *haus*. Rebecca stormed past her just as she kicked the snow from her boot, letting the door slam behind her.

"What's the matter?"

Her *schwester's* upper lip sneered. "You'll find out soon enough."

Emma pulled the screen door open while watching Rebecca over her shoulder.

Her *datt* sat in the same spot as she left him earlier, but this time he sat with his arms folded over his chest.

"Is there a problem?" she asked as she hung up her coat and unwrapped the scarf from her neck.

He held his hand out in her direction. "Hand it over."

She didn't even need to ask what he was referring to and took the phone from her apron pocket.

His large, calloused hands engulfed the phone, and only a small sliver could be seen beneath his fingers. "I'll not have the likes of this in my *haus*."

A wave of emotion spilled over on her cheeks at his tone.

"Where did you get that?"

"Daniel."

"Exactly why I'll side with Levi on this one. No reason you need to associate yourself with him. The boy promised me last year he wouldn't influence his worldly ways on you. He can't be trusted."

"But *Datt*."

"But *Datt* nothing. As long as you're under my roof, I expect you to abide by the rules of the *Ordnung*."

As she walked away, he added, "I'll be telling Matthew the same thing when he returns."

Chapter 10

Sugarcreek

A soft knock on her bedroom door forced Emma to sit up and wipe the moisture from her face. "Come in."

Anna peeked around the door frame. "Are you okay?"

"How did *Datt* find out about my phone?"

"Rebecca went out to feed the cats and heard you."

"What does she have against me? I only use it to call Daniel. This time I was calling Nathan and Marie."

Anna took a seat beside her on the bed. "I'm not sure what her problem is, but she'll do anything to get you in trouble. I tried to talk to her, but you know how she gets. For sure and certain, she thinks *datt* treats you differently. I don't see it."

Emma reached over and patted her arm. "Thanks for sticking up for me."

"That's what *schwester's* do. And don't give Rebecca too much mind; she'll come around sooner or later. I'd try to stay out of her way if I were you."

"I'll stay out of her way, alright. I think I'm going to go to Sugarcreek to visit with my mom some, and Daniel could use a change of scenery."

"How are you going to get there?"

"I'm expecting he'll drive me."

"Ohhhhh... *Datt's* not going to like that."

"Probably why I'm not going to tell him."

"Oh, I wish you wouldn't have told me. You know I can't lie."

"I'm sorry, maybe I shouldn't have told you, but I think I'm causing more grief around here than good."

Anna's voice cracked. "Please don't go. What will I do without you?"

"You and Rebecca have things under control."

"That's not the point. *Mamm*, now you."

Emma pulled Anna into her arms. "I feel it too. Everything's different now that *Mamm's* gone."

~

Emma waited until everyone had long gone to bed before tiptoeing downstairs, carefully avoiding the steps that creaked. The phone her *datt* used in his shop to deal with his English customers would pave her way. The moon bounced light off the white ground as the snow crunched beneath her feet. She stopped only once to look back at the darkened house. An emptiness filled her, and a twinge of guilt made her second guess leaving without saying goodbye. She set the small suitcase down at her feet and found the hidden key to the door and headed to the phone. Her stomach churned as the phone rang on the other end. Daniel was so unpredictable these days she wasn't sure which Daniel would answer.

"Hello."

"Daniel, it's Emma."

"Why are you calling from your *datt's* shop? Where's your phone?"

"It doesn't matter. Can you pick me up?"

"Now?"

"Yes, if it wouldn't be too much trouble. "

"Where do you want to go?"

"I want to go to Nathan and Marie's."

"Tonight?"

"Not necessarily tonight, but I was hoping you could take me."

"Where do you want to go?"

"I thought I could go back to your hotel room for the night."

"This is no place for you."

"Daniel, please. I don't care about the room. It will be fine."

"I'll be there in fifteen minutes."

Before hanging up, she quickly instructed. "Don't pull in the driveway. I'll wait about ten minutes, and then I'll walk to the road and wait for you."

She put the phone back in its cradle and picked up a pen and pad from the desk. She positioned the small flashlight on the desk to illuminate the notepad.

Datt,

I love you and will always feel honored you chose to bring me to Willow Springs and raise me as your own. You've molded me into the person I've become, and I will forever be grateful for the childhood you gave me. I know it's hard for you to understand my need to have a relationship with Daniel, and I know if I want one, I cannot do that here. He is family, and I can't turn my back on him, especially when he needs me the most. I'm returning to Sugarcreek. I'll be staying with Marie and Nathan.

Please forgive me for leaving in the middle of the night without a proper goodbye. I couldn't bear the agony in your eyes once again.

Forever and always, your daughter,

Emma

She folded the note in half, wrote his name on it, and left it on his desk. Memories filled her mind, and she choked back a sob on her walk to the end of the driveway. She was grieving the loss of her *Mamm* and mourning the loss of life as she knew it. The realization that *Gott* had other plans hit her hard, and she struggled to free the cry embedded in the back of her throat. An uneasiness covered her with each step leaving behind a trail of broken dreams. What she thought would be her life clearly was not what *Gott* had in mind. She prayed as she took the final steps from one life into another.

Gott, please help me trust in your plan. Help me reach Daniel and allow us both to find our way in this life you've put in front of us. Amen

Lights crested the hill, and Daniel slowed to a stop beside her. With a gloved hand on the door handle, she took one last look toward her childhood home. The dampness on her cheeks turned cold, much like her heart, as she climbed inside.

It only took a second for Daniel to ask. "Are you sure you want to do this?"

She slid the brown leather case on the seat between them. "Willow Springs doesn't hold what we both need. Our family is in Sugarcreek, and it's time we face that."

Daniel pulled back onto the road, and his voice changed. "I'll take you back, but don't count on me staying."

Emma slipped her fingers from her mittens and folded her hands on her lap. "I beg to differ. I think if you stop running from your past and face it head-on, you'll find you need what our grandfather has to offer."

"I'm not so sure about that, but I'm in no mood to argue with you." He turned up the radio and drove back into town.

Without realizing where he was going, Emma sat quietly, trying to find words to convince him otherwise. She could tell he was in no mood to talk since he used the radio to silence her words.

102

He turned into his parent's house and shut the engine off. "You can stay here for the night, and I'll come for you in the morning. They're expecting you."

With an uneasiness in her voice she said, "I'd rather stay with you."

"As I said before, my hotel room is no place for you. I'll be back first thing in the morning."

He took her suitcase from the seat and carried it to the front door. She followed him and stood beside him as he opened it. He didn't follow her inside but raised a hand to his waiting parents. "Thank you. I'll be back bright and early in the morning."

For a split second, she thought she saw a shimmer of the old Daniel when he greeted his parents. Before she could comment, the door shut, and he was gone.

Mr. Miller took her suitcase from her hand, and Mrs. Miller guided her to the kitchen. "I made a pot of herbal tea to help you sleep. When we travel, I love to have a cup before bed; it helps me rest in a strange environment."

Mr. Miller headed up the stairs. "I'll put your bag in the first room to the right."

Before she had a chance to answer, Mrs. Miller had her in the kitchen and at the table pouring hot liquid into a porcelain teacup.

"It's nice to finally meet you. Daniel told us so much about you." Mrs. Miller studied her face. "You favor him. I think it's the eyes. Yep, I'm sure of it."

Mr. Miller came through the door and sat beside her. "I think I'll have a cup of that as well."

The older woman scurried to the cupboard as Mr. Miller said, "I think going back to Sugarcreek is what the both of you need."

Emma took a sip of her tea. "I think so too."

Mrs. Miller piped in. "Daniel needs to get away from those boys he's been hanging out with. He never did such things when we lived in Sugarcreek."

Mr. Miller stirred sugar into his cup. "He knows right from wrong, and he has free will to make his own choices. I wouldn't blame those young men. He could have easily said no or found other company." He nibbled on a cookie off the plate in front of him. "No, he needs to own up to his mistakes, and we don't need to be blaming anyone but Daniel."

Emma listened and wondered if he might understand the extent of his bad behavior.

Mrs. Miller clanked her spoon on the side of her cup to make a point. "All I know is I'm glad he's taking you back to Sugarcreek. He needs to get away from Willow Springs."

Mr. Miller looked Emma's way. "How much did Daniel tell you about his past?"

"Not much. Only that he spent time in foster homes before you adopted him. He never seems like he wants to talk about that much, so I've never pressed him on it."

The color drained from his face. "You need to know what he's up against. He suffered some abuse and it left scars that are not so easily forgotten. We sent him to counseling for years, and we thought he'd worked through the worst of it. I can see now that some of those memories have made their way back into his life."

The sheer size of Mr. Miller seemed to shrink as he recalled the depth of his son's pain. Emma could tell by listening to the older gentleman he had a love for his adoptive son that ran as deep as any biological child could bring. His voice softened as he spoke. "No ten-year-old should be subjected to those things."

Emma's heart ached as she read between the lines of Mr. Miller's words. He didn't say it out loud, but she could only imagine what he was referring to.

Emma whispered. "I had no idea."

Mrs. Miller wiped the end of her nose with a tissue she pulled from beneath the sleeve of her gray sweater. "It breaks my heart every time I think of it, and here to find out his own grandfather could have saved him from all of that."

Things started to click in Emma's head. That was the reason he was so angry. It was no excuse to drink so much or hurt Katie, but she did understand.

Mr. Miller straightened up in his chair. "God always has a plan. We might not see it amid our pain, but it's there. I strongly believe He puts people in our paths for a reason. If only for a minute, they're strategically placed to impact us in one way or another. Nothing happens in life by chance, and it's up to us to follow the path that will best glorify Him, even through difficult situations."

Emma ran her finger along the rim of her cup. "I don't understand. How can Daniel's abuse be something from *Gott?"*

"I'm not saying God orchestrated the event to take place, but he can turn bad into good."

Emma asked, "But how?"

"By teaching us things like forgiveness and grace. Daniel's got a lot of built-up anger he needs to deal with, and until he learns to forgive as the Lord instructs us to do, he'll never get past this."

Mrs. Miller reached over and laid her hand on Emma's arm. "So, you see, my dear, we think by making him go back to Sugarcreek, he can face some of those obstacles face to face."

Emma shifted in her chair. "He says he's not staying."

Mr. Miller carried his cup to the sink. "I think a call to Nathan in the morning might fix that. Since he lost his job at the mill, I'm sure his money is getting low. I'm certain a job offer might encourage him to stick around for a little bit."

Emma handed her cup to Mrs. Miller's outstretched hand. "I called Nathan today, and he mentioned he needed help at the stables."

Mr. Miller stood and pushed out his chair. "He's always looked up to Nathan, and it might be what the boy needs. One last thing before I head on up to bed. Make sure he stops by and sees the Yoder girl before he leaves town. He doesn't need the guilt of that hanging over his head, and I'm praying she'll offer him forgiveness, so he knows how it feels."

A small gasp escaped Emma's lips. "You know?"

"I do, and even though I'm appalled, he needs to apologize."

"I'm not sure her family will let her see him."

"Regardless, he needs to try."

~~

Mrs. Miller had breakfast waiting on the table long before Emma made her way back down to the kitchen the next morning. Daniel sat next to his father at the table and smiled her way when she entered the room.

"I hope I didn't keep you all waiting. The bed was so comfortable I didn't want to leave."

"No problem, my dear, we've eaten, but I saved you some. I'll warm it up for you."

"Please, don't go to any trouble."

"It's no trouble at all; it will only take me a minute. Sit and make yourself a cup of tea."

Daniel took the last sip of his coffee and said, "I'm ready to go as soon as you finish your breakfast." He glanced at his father and back at Emma. "I have one stop to make before we head out."

Emma looked toward Mr. Miller, and he winked at her. She knew the stop would be Katie's.

Daniel's parents walked them to the door and hugged them both as they left. Once Emma settled into her seat and fastened her belt, she looked back toward the house and waved at the older couple. They were good people and she smiled at the tenderness they showed her.

"I like your parents."

"Yeah, they grow on you, don't they?" He looked back fondly and waved goodbye. "If it weren't for them, my life would have turned out much worse, I'm sure."

"Your dad told me something last night I can't stop thinking about."

"What's that?"

"That *Gott* puts people in our paths for a purpose."

Replying in a short snicker he said. "I guess my purpose is to be your chauffeur?"

"No, seriously. Think about it. Look how *Gott* etched our lives together in a complete circle sending us back to the place we started. Only *Gott* knew to send your parents to live in Willow Springs. Who else could orchestrate you and Matthew to become friends, and who could weave a plan that led you back to me? You can't tell me that wasn't all from *Gott*."

"I suppose, but don't forget I'm not staying; I'm driving you there and coming right back."

She pointed in the back. "If so, why did you pack a bag?"

"A storm might come up, and I'll get stranded somewhere."

"I hope you at least stay for a few days and visit with Mom and Nathan. I'm sure they will enjoy it."

"I won't promise anything, but I'll think about it."

Daniel slowed and turned onto Mystic Mill Road before asking. "I need to talk to Katie. Got any ideas on how to make that happen?"

Emma kept her eyes focused on the snow-covered road and said softly. "I know what you did."

"Then you know why I need to talk to her."

She pointed to the clearing on the side of the road. "Park there. I'll go to the house and see if I can convince her to take a walk with me. I'll be back shortly."

Emma pulled her coat snugly around her middle and tipped her head to block the wind that pushed up under her thick bonnet. Saying goodbye to her best friend and their plans were about as hard as saying goodbye to *Mamm*. She and Katie had been friends since before they could walk, and at times she felt closer to her than she did to her own *schwesters*.

She held on to the railing leading up the snow-covered stairs of the Yoder porch. Standing in front of the baby blue door, she took a deep breath before knocking. Behind the closed door, she heard the shuffle of feet on the polished floors heading her way.

The door opened, and Katie greeted her with a smile, pulling her in out of the cold. "What a nice surprise. What are you doing out so early?"

"I was hoping you'd take a walk with me. I need to talk to you about something."

"A walk? It's cold out. We can go up to my room if you want."

Emma looked toward the kitchen, where Katie's parents sat at the table and leaned in closer. "I'd rather take a walk if you don't mind. Bundle up, I promise we won't be long."

Katie mouthed, "Is everything okay?"

"*Jah*, I just need to talk to you outside."

"Alright, give me a minute. Let me go upstairs and put a pair of tights on under my dress."

"Hurry, I don't have much time."

Katie furrowed her forehead and ran up the stairs taking them two at a time at her friend's request.

Ruth hollered from the kitchen. "Emma, come in; no need to stand at the door."

Emma slipped her boots off but didn't remove her coat or bonnet and followed Ruth's voice.

"How's your *datt* doing?"

Emma swallowed hard at the thought of how he might be doing at that very moment. Most likely, he'd found her note and wasn't doing well at all.

"He's okay. Some days are harder than others. Thank goodness he still has orders to process to keep his mind busy. I think it's worse in the evenings when they would normally sit in the front room together."

Levi pushed his chair away from the table and bent over to slip on his boots. "I have a few errands to run in town this afternoon. I'll stop by and check on him. How about you tell him I'll be stopping by later?"

Emma didn't answer but dropped her head in silence.

Katie brushed by her and put on her coat and scarf. "I'm ready."

Ruth stood at the table clearing breakfast dishes and asked, "For heaven's sake, girls, where are you going on such a chilly morning? I wouldn't say it's a day for a walk."

Katie looked toward Emma and then back at her *mamm*. "We won't be gone long. I'll work on that quilt when I return."

They didn't wait for Ruth to answer before heading to the door. Once outside, Katie grabbed Emma's arm and asked, "What's so important and what's with that look on your face? I can tell you have something weighing on your mind, so spill it."

Emma headed down the steps and guided Katie to the driveway. She kept a tight hold on her arm, keeping her from bolting the other way. "Daniel wants to talk to you."

Katie dug her heels in the snow and shook her head back and forth. "Oh, please, Emma, no. I'm not ready to talk to him."

She pulled her closer and forced her to walk with her. "But you have to. We're leaving."

"Stop! What do you mean you're leaving? Where are you going?"

"We're going back to Sugarcreek."

In a long-drawn-out whine Katie said, "You can't! What about the bakery?"

"I'm sorry to disappoint you, but I need to go back, and Daniel should leave Willow Springs."

Katie pulled at Emma's sleeve. "Why does he want to talk to me?"

Emma gently held up Katie's wrist, "I'm sure about this."

"Has he been drinking?"

"No, not this morning as much as I can tell, and not last night either. He seems more like himself, or at least more himself than he's been in months."

"I'm not so sure about this."

Emma pleaded. "Please, he needs your forgiveness."

Katie stopped and pulled Emma back. "It's not that I can't forgive him. I can do that because that's what *Gott* tells us to do. But I can't forget that he hurt me, and that part scares me. What if I give him grace and it happens again?"

Emma took both of her hands and turned to face her. "I don't know what the answer to that is. All I know is that he should find out what forgiveness feels like so he could offer Melvin the same. Please, Katie, you're my only hope. *Gott* would want you to show him what it feels like to be truly forgiven. This is what we've been raised to do our whole life ...forgive as *Gott* forgave us."

As soon as they walked over the ridge, Daniel came into view. He flipped the collar of his jean jacket and buried his hands deep in his pockets.

Katie stopped directly in front of him, and Emma walked past and climbed back into the truck. Whatever her *bruder* had to say to Katie was none of her concern, and she took her cue to leave them alone.

~~

Daniel kicked a clump of snow at his feet before looking into Katie's eyes. "I don't know what to say other than I'm sorry. In my right mind, I would never hurt you." He shifted his weight and rested on the warm engine. "I don't blame you if you never want to talk to me again."

Katie's bluebird eyes and the dark wisps of hair fluttering in the wind from beneath her blue scarf left him speechless. He focused his eyes on hers, hoping and praying she would say something, anything.

In a soft, almost inaudible voice, she said, "I don't like who you become when you're drinking."

He stuttered. "For what it's worth, I don't like who I become either."

He stepped closer, longing to shorten the distance between them. When he did, she stepped back.

He held his hands out, palms up, praying she'd take them. He anxiously waited for her hands to mold to his. When she finally laid her hand on top of his, he removed her mitten and pushed the sleeve of her jacket up. The yellowed fingerprints were like a sharp sword to his heart, and he brought her wrist to his lips. He closed his eyes and whispered through tortured breath, "Please forgive me."

The warmth of her skin against his lips added a level of emotion he couldn't control. He hadn't shed a tear since he was ten, but at that moment, the thought of what he'd done overcame him. He pulled her into his chest and rested his chin on top of her head. "Please tell me you can forgive me."

Katie wrapped her arms around his middle and tipped her head back to meet his eyes. "Not only forgiven but forgotten."

He placed his finger under her chin, turned her head, and kissed her cheek. "I'm going back to Sugarcreek. I need to take care of some things." He took a minute to inhale her scent. "May I write you?"

She took a step back but held his hands. "I'm not so sure my parents will allow a letter to pass through their fingers from you, but maybe if you tuck one inside of Emma's, it might get to me."

"Hopefully, one day, I'll earn their trust back. For now, I'll be happy with whatever small part of yourself you can give me."

She squeezed his fingertips. "Promise me you'll get help. Drowning yourself in a bottle won't do you any good."

"I think I'm learning that the hard way."

She pulled her hands away, put on her mittens, and turned to leave. She waved to Emma. "Take care of yourself, Daniel Miller, and take care of that girl. She's the best friend I've ever had, and I expect a letter from you both soon."

Daniel stood watching her disappear over the ridge. He wasn't sure if there could be a future for him and the sweet girl from Willow Springs, but first and foremost he needed to face his past before he could plan his future.

He climbed back into the warmth and held his chilled fingers over the dashboard. Without taking his eyes off the spot where Katie dotted the landscape, he asked his sister. "Are you ready to go home?"

Chapter 11

Church

Emma flipped the calendar on the *doddi haus* kitchen wall to a new month and circled March thirty-first with a red marker.

"Just think, only one more month, and you'll be Mrs. Nathan Boutcright."

Marie smiled up at her daughter as she sat at the kitchen table, mending a pair of trousers.

"Aren't you excited?" Emma asked.

"Excited? More like scared to death."

"But why? It's written all over your face how you feel about Nathan. Why would you be nervous?"

"Easy for you to say. You were raised Amish, and even though my mother was Mennonite, there's a big difference. I'm still learning to speak the language, and the bishop still has a few more baptismal sessions to go through. It's a big step."

"A big step for sure and certain, and one you fit so easily into."

Marie examined her stitches and held the seam closer to the oil lamp hung over the table. "I'll never be good at this, but I can make a mean meatloaf, and we all know the way to a man's heart is through his stomach. Thank goodness it's not through these tiny stitches."

Emma walked closer to the light and took the pants from her mother's hands. "Here, let me help."

Marie stood and rubbed her lower back and walked to the window overlooking the garden. Remnants of last summer still stood in the frozen ground. "How about I leave the sewing to you? You're much better at it."

Marie sifted through the stack of mail on the counter, flipping through the letters and advertisements. "I swear if these companies who try to sell Nathan new products would show up in person, they'd have a better chance. If I've learned anything about my future husband, it's he'd much rather do business with a handshake than a heap of paper."

Marie tucked the mail under her arm and pulled her sweater tight around her middle. "If you have those pants under control, I'm going to walk this mail over to Nathan."

"I'm okay. Go enjoy yourself. I bet the *kinner* are in bed by now; why don't you spend some time with Nathan? I'm sure he'd enjoy it."

"I might do that. There's a letter from Katie on the counter for you and Daniel. When you're through, and if you want, you can take it to him in the loft."

Emma pulled the knot through the dark broadcloth and snipped the end before folding the pants and leaving them on the table. She picked up the letter addressed to herself and carried it to the rocking chair in the living room. The small *doddi haus,* across the yard from Nathan's had become their temporary home, until Marie married at the end of the month. Once that happened, they would both move into the big house.

She slid her finger along the flap to release the letter and pulled out the pink-lined sheet meant for her and the blue folded one sealed with tape for Daniel. It had become a weekly ritual that she looked forward to. The look on Daniel's face when she delivered his hidden letter always brought a smile to her face. Emma held the letter up to the light to read it more closely. Katie's handwriting, a perfect script, made her miss her even more.

Emma,

Winter is never-ending these days; the temperatures are so frigid my nose freezes when I feed the chickens. Remember a few years ago when Samuel tied that yellow ribbon to your coop? I thought about that the other day and had to laugh to myself. We had so much fun trying to figure it all out. Such simple times that I miss.

Samuel's not been himself, but I don't need to tell you the reason why. Edna's been stopping by; she says she's coming to see me, but we both know who she hopes to visit. I don't know what's going on there, some day's he acts like he's excited to see her, and then other days, he seems annoyed. Are you sure you can't work things out with him? I'm sorry, I shouldn't tell you about such things, but I want you to know how I see it. Isn't that what best friends are for?

More than once, I felt the urge to run across the field to share something with you, but then I remember you aren't here. I sure do miss you.

Emma stopped to wipe the pools from her eyes.

I saw Rebecca and Anna at the market yesterday, and I asked how your datt was doing. They both said he was doing well but still missed your mamm. They mentioned his orders had picked up, and he'd been spending a lot of time out in the shop. I questioned them both on the package of celery seeds they had in their cart, and they both smiled. I assume there is a wedding in the mix for fall. My guess is Matthew and Sarah are planning an announcement. I'm dying to know, so please don't keep me waiting in the dark too long.

The bakery is coming right along. Samuel and Datt have been working long hours getting the kitchen set up and ready to open before the strawberry season. Edna offered to help me bake pies, but I'm not so sure she's the right person to fill your spot. Again, I think she's coming around because of Samuel.

For now, I think Mamm's going to help me, or at least until you figure out how long you're going to stay in Sugarcreek. My heart yearns for us to run it together, and I'm not ready to let go of that dream yet.

I hope this letter finds you well and don't forget to write me back soon and tell me what you've heard about Matthew and Sarah. I haven't seen Rebecca or Anna leave the singeon with anyone special, so it has to be Matthew. Who else could it be?

May God bless you and your time in Sugarcreek.

Your friend, Katie

Emma tucked the letter back in the envelope and left it on the stand near the chair. She slipped her sweater around her shoulders and opened the door, grabbing the lantern on her way to the stables. A pungent odor tickled her nose as she headed up the stairs. Daniel lay stretched out on his bed, shaking his foot in beat to whatever was playing through his earbuds. He didn't hear her approach, and she reached out and tapped his shoulder. He removed the music from his ears, rolled over, and sat up.

"Lucky day for me," he said as he pointed to the blue paper in her hand. "I take it that's for me?"

"It sure is, but I'm holding it for ransom until you answer a couple of questions."

"And what would that be?"

"What do you know about Matthew and Sarah?"

Daniel's upper lip twitched. "I can't imagine what you're referring to."

"Oh, come on, Daniel, I know you better than that. I saw you got a letter from Matthew the other day."

"I'd say anything that Matthew shares with me is private."

Emma crossed her arms over her chest. "Katie mentioned seeing Rebecca and Anna at the Mercantile and for some unknown reason they had a stash of celery seed in their cart."

"Who knows, maybe it's for Rebecca or Anna."

"Come on, you can do better than that."

"Are you going to tease me with that letter all day?"

"I told you I'm holding it for ransom until you tell me what's going on with Matthew."

"If you have questions for your brother, you need to ask him yourself." Daniel reached up and snatched the letter from Emma's hand and tucked it under his thigh. "Anything else on your mind?"

"Only that Mom wants you to go to church with us tomorrow."

Daniel stiffened his back. "Isn't it enough I agreed to stay to help Nathan?"

"Yes, but that's only half the battle you're fighting."

"Look, I have no desire to face Shetler."

"One of these days, you're going to have to get whatever's on your chest about our grandfather out in the open. You're never going to get past all of this until you face him."

Daniel stood and walked to the window before he turned to face his sister. "I have a lot of animosity toward that man, and I'm not so sure I could be cordial if I did see him."

"But can't you see he wants to make amends?"

"I'd say it's long past time for me to accept an apology,"

Emma picked up the lantern and asked, "Didn't Katie teach you anything? Look how easy it was for her to forgive you, and yet you still can't see past your pain to offer the same kind of grace to Melvin."

Emma headed to the door but stopped and turned abruptly. "Give it to *Gott*. That's what you need to do."

"Again, I'll ask. Where was He when I needed Him?"

Emma opened the door but not before repeating it louder. "Give it to *Gott*."

Daniel turned back toward the darkened window as he listened to Emma's footsteps on the stairs. All of the sudden he heard; *"Forgive him. I do not say to you seven times, but seventy times seven."* Daniel turned from the window expecting to see a figure in the room. Shaking his head, he tried to make sense of the voice, and in an instant, there it was again. *"Go to him. Let him help you heal. It's time."*

Daniel sat on the bed, rested his elbows on his knees, and buried his head in his hands. Could he offer the one man who turned his back on him, grace and forgiveness? He cried out to God, *"How can you expect me to just forgive and forget? He turned his back on my own father, on me, and on Emma. How do you expect me to forget that? Now you want me to go to his church? The church he chose over me?"*

The sudden urge for a drink hung over his head like a dark cloud. It took all he had to fight the desire.

~~

The bright and sunny Sunday greeted Emma on the porch as she waited for Nathan to maneuver the family buggy around the front of the *haus*. She missed her home church, but she enjoyed getting to know her birth family and the people in her grandfather's *g'may*. Amos and Rachel's happy squeals from across the yard pulled her away from her thoughts.

Rachel hollered, "Emma are you coming?"

She followed the sound of Rachel's voice to the buggy, all while looking over her shoulder, hoping Daniel would join them. Before climbing in the buggy, her mother laid a hand on her arm and muttered, "I take it you didn't have any luck convincing Daniel to join us today?"

118

"No, but I won't give up hope yet."

Emma took a seat in the back between Amos and Rachel and settled into listening to them explain about the squirrels they saw in the bird feeder. Nathan wrapped hot bricks in towels to keep their toes warm, but the chilly March morning made for a brisk five-mile ride to Bishop Shetler's home. This would be the first time she'd visit her *Doddi* Melvin and *Mommi* Lillian's house. Part of her yearned for the closeness of grandparents. Her *mamm's* parents passed when she was five, and she never got a chance to know her *datt's* parents.

Nathan skillfully handled the buggy on the icy roads and pulled up beside Shetler's red dairy barn. A row of black-topped buggies were parked between the *haus* and red building. A team of young boys were unhitching the horses and leading them to the pasture. Amos and Rachel were anxious to run off with their friends and practically jumped out of the buggy once it stopped. Marie reached back and took the pan of fry pies from Emma's lap and climbed out herself.

Emma's breath made a circle around her face as she followed Marie to the line forming near the farmhouse's side door. Without saying a word, she fell into place behind the line of women waiting to be greeted inside. A small flutter reminded her this was her birth *datt's* childhood home, and she would soon step foot into the same kitchen that had nourished his young soul.

Marie stopped sharply in front of her and turned. "You're awful quiet. Are you okay?"

"*Jah*, I think so. I'm a little nervous about going inside. The thought of being here and knowing this is where my *datt* was raised is getting to me."

Marie's face had the same faraway look and she leaned in closer so only Emma could hear. "I was here only once, but I didn't feel welcome. Those memories have been playing with me all morning. I'm with

119

Nathan now, but I have to agree it's a bit unnerving when I think about how our life took a full circle …right back to where it all started."

"Do you think Lillian is nervous as well?" Emma asked.

Marie moved closer and whispered, "She stopped over to the house a few times, and we've had a chance to talk things through. I even had a couple of visits from Melvin, so I know where we stand."

Marie shifted the dish in her hands. "Nervous? I don't think so. I think I'd explain it more as hopeful. They so badly want to make up for lost time with you and Daniel if you let them."

The line moved forward, and within minutes Emma found herself face-to-face with her *mommi*. A nervous smiled creased the old woman's face, and Emma stopped, letting her kiss her. Lillian kept her hands on Emma's arms longer than expected and squeezed them before releasing her hands. The hint of mint and rose petals filled Emma's nose as the older woman placed her fingertips on the side of her cheek. No louder than a whisper, she said, "I am so happy to see you again. I prayed you would join us today."

Emma smiled and moved as the line behind her edged her on. She ran her hand along the oak table as she passed, trying to imagine which seat was her father's. She wished she could sit close to Marie but followed the line of young girls her age to the back of the room. Within minutes of finding a seat, the ministers, along with her *doddi*, Bishop Shetler, made their way around the room, greeting each person. The men waited on the porch until all the women had found a seat on one side of the room. Like in her home church, the ministers headed upstairs to pray and prepare for the sermon as someone in the back of the room started to sing the first few words of the first song. The slow and steady words relaxed Emma's nervousness, and she let her birth *datt's* family home comfort her.

~~

Daniel parked at the end of Shetler's driveway and contemplated if he would walk the remaining distance on foot. He gripped the steering wheel and dropped his head, willing himself to step outside and open himself to the unknown. Praying God would give him the strength he needed, he opened his eyes and caught the sight of an envelope on the floor. With his name printed across the front, the familiar white paper tied his stomach in a knot. While the messages inside were always spot on, the mystery of where and how they appeared left him uneasy about the sender.

Daniel,
This is where you belong. Don't turn your back on what God is trying to show you.
"Get rid of all bitterness, rage, and anger, brawling and slander, along with every form of malice. Be kind and compassionate to one another, forgiving each other, just as in Christ God forgave you." Ephesians 4:31-32
JS

Before he lost his nerve, he opened the door to both his heart and the cold. The frozen ground creaked under his heavy boots as he made his way to the sounds penetrating through the walls of his grandparent's house. He stopped on the porch, but instead of opening the door, he pushed a row of hats to the side and took a seat on a bench. For the next hour, he sat in the cold, listening to the voices from inside and trying to find the will to push the past from his mind. Movement on the end of the porch alerted his attention to a man, not much older than himself, moving toward him. The man stopped short of the front door and said, "You won't find your way home sitting out here."

There was something about the man that offered him comfort, and without saying a word, he stood and followed him inside. The warmth of the room was inviting, and Daniel took a seat next to the man who felt oddly familiar. His eyes skimmed the clean-shaven man and tried to place where he had seen him before. Maybe he was a customer of Nathan's, or perhaps he'd met him when he attended church last summer. He'd have to find out later, but at that moment, his grandfather took his place at the front of the room, pulling his attention away from the stranger. As the bishop stood and turned to face the room, he stopped and locked eyes with Daniel. When the older gentleman failed to start a sentence, the room spun and followed their bishop's gaze.

Bishop Shetler cleared his throat and began. "If a man has a hundred sheep and one of them goes astray, will he not leave the ninety-nine in the hills and go in search of the stray? I say to you, he rejoices more over that one than he would over the ninety-nine."

For the next hour, Daniel sat and listened to his grandfather share his message about the lost sheep. Often fixating his eyes and his words on Daniel until his voice drifted in another direction. It hadn't been the first time Daniel had attended a three-hour service, and he knew enough to follow the lead of each ritual. Indicating the last prayer, he turned and knelt in front of the bench, closing his eyes and praying to put forgiveness in his heart.

Church ended and he looked around the room until he located Emma and his mother. They stood flanked by Lillian and Emma's Aunt Anna Mae. Not wanting to interrupt, he proceeded outside with the rest of the men. A few men stayed back to convert the benches into tables as the women set the room up for a light lunch.

Nathan and Amos walked up beside him just as he was about to address the man at his side. But the man had left, and he only caught a glimpse of him as he walked down the steps of the porch. He turned his attention back to Nathan, who had slapped a friendly greeting to his shoulder. "This is a good place to start."

Daniel glanced to the figure of the man who was disappearing out of sight. "I suppose so, but I don't think I'm staying."

Amos looked up. "But why? We didn't have lunch yet and Marie brought fry pies."

Nathan responded, "The boy has a point. Leaving before having one of Marie's apple fry pies is a sin indeed."

Daniel tousled the boy's hair. "Okay, you talked me into it."

He trailed Nathan after taking one last look at the figure disappearing into the landscape.

Chapter 12
Forgiveness

Lillian noticed her husband from across the room, staring out the front window. He had aged in the last eight months. She was certain it was from admitting to Daniel and Emma the part he played in their life. She excused herself from the conversation she was having with Anna Mae and weaved her way through the room. Once she made it to her husband's side, she whispered, "Go to him."

Melvin didn't take his eyes off the group of men walking across the yard. "At this point, I'm glad he came. I don't want to push him away."

Lillian touched his arm, "I'm sure he's expecting you to speak to him."

She moved even closer and talked in a hushed tone. "*Gott* forgives you. When are you going to forgive yourself?"

Melvin looked down at his wife's gray eyes, lifted her hand, and patted it ever so gently. He took his black wool hat off the peg by the living room door and positioned it snugly to his head. With one long sweep, he ran his fingers through his long graying beard and took in a deep breath as he opened the door. Each stride across the yard brought him closer to facing the hurt and anger he saw in his grandsons' face. Over the years, he tried reasoning with himself on why he turned his back on his son's family. There were so many things he wasn't sure he could explain himself.

He had tried to make amends in his own way by fighting for Marie's early release and placing Emma with Jacob and Stella Byler. Even getting Daniel away from the foster care system and into Mr. and Mrs. Miller's arms was his doing. More than anything, they had no way of knowing he'd spent the previous twenty-one years with unbearable guilt of turning his back on his eldest son. It was hard being the bishop. People looked up to him and scrutinized his family like no other in the community. In his own mind, he was protecting them. Instead, it put a wedge between the thing that he valued most …family.

The pain of turning his back on his own kin consumed his every waking moment. The one thought that haunted him was if he couldn't save his own son from worldly ways, how would he ever raise Daniel and Emma to be *Gott*-fearing Amish children? More than once over the years, he cried out to *Gott,* asking Him to forgive him.

He stood outside the barn door, trying to brace himself for the hatred in Daniel's eyes. It only took a second to scan the room and find the spitting image of his eldest son. Daniel's sandy-colored hair flipped up around his baseball cap, pulled tight to his head. As if history was repeating itself, a vision flashed before his eyes of the last time he'd spoken to his son.

It was the day, acting as the bishop, he delivered the shunning news. He stiffened his back and pushed the memory from his mind and walked to where Daniel stood. Stopping only for a moment to shake the hand of a few church members before continuing. He inched closer and held his breath until he stopped within a foot of the boy, who was now a man.

"Daniel."

"Bishop."

"Melvin is fine."

There was a chill in the air, not so much from the temperature outside but from Daniel's icy glare.

125

"I'd appreciate it if you stuck around for a while today."

Daniel tucked his hands in his pocket and shuffled on one foot. "What for?"

"I have a few things I'd like to talk to you about."

"I'm not too sure I'm ready to listen to what you might have to say."

His demeanor made the hair stand up on the back of his neck. His stubbornness reminded him so much like his eldest, along with his uncanny resemblance.

"I'll leave that up to you, but my invitation stands."

Daniel watched as his grandfather turned to leave. There was a softness in his eyes he couldn't help but notice. Was it regret or a plea for forgiveness? Could the man be sorry for all he did? He stood in the corner until all the men had headed back to the house to eat. Without realizing Nathan had stayed behind, Nathan laid his hand on his shoulder. "You don't want to believe it, but the man does care about you."

"If that's the case, he's done a poor job of showing it."

"Daniel, you have no idea what that man did for you and your family."

Forming multiple creases across his forehead, he asked, "Do you know something you're not telling me?"

"I'm not saying everything he's done would be the way I would've handled things. However, I realize the responsibility of being a bishop comes with a high price. Sometimes in life, *Gott* puts us on a path that is meant to teach us something. Whether it be forgiveness or to look to Him for help. I believe people cross our paths for more than one reason. *Gott* always has a plan, even if it doesn't line up to what you thought it should be. Or, in this case, what Melvin figured it would be. But for whatever reason, you're here, he's here, and you're crossing a path only *Gott* could have seen."

"I suppose so. You are not the first person to tell me that."

Nathan slapped him on the back, "Sometimes it takes more than one person to get through our thick skulls. Come on, how about we go get some lunch?"

Daniel followed Nathan back to the house and wondered how strange it was that Nathan had said almost his father's exact words. How was it he kept hearing the same words over and over again? He started to believe God was genuinely trying to talk to him. Maybe it was time he began to open not only his ears, but his heart as well.

~~

Daniel lingered until the last buggy had pulled from his grandfather's driveway before heading back to the house. He stayed outside as long as he could, helping each last church member hook up their buggy to head home. For the past two hours, he agonized over the conversation that was yet to come. He knocked the snow off his boots on the top step, took off his hat, and brushed the last of the hay off his jeans. Before he had a chance to knock on the door, it swung open, and his grandmother stood in the doorway.

"Please come in."

Daniel slipped his boots off before following Lillian to the kitchen. He hung his jacket on the peg and laid his baseball cap on top of his boots. The benches were stacked in the church wagon and the room had been turned back into a home. His grandfather sat at the head of the table and motioned him to take a seat.

"Thank you for staying," his grandfather murmured.

Lillian placed a plate of cookies on the table and poured hot water into a waiting mug. She topped off Melvin's cup before taking a seat.

Daniel waited and busied himself with adding sugar to his cup before Melvin took in a long breath and folded his arms across his chest. "We have much to talk about."

Melvin reached up and ran his hand through his long beard and sat back in his chair. "Is there anything you'd like to ask me first?"

Before Daniel had a chance to even weigh his words, he asked, "Why?"

Melvin cleared his throat. "Not that it makes any difference now, but at the time, I felt I'd do you *kinner* more justice finding you other families."

"Why on earth would you think that was better than raising us yourself?"

Melvin stuttered. "I had an image to uphold."

Daniel tried to control the urge to raise his voice and clenched his teeth before responding. "That's what I don't understand."

Lillian's soft tone added a calmness to the air. "Being a bishop is like a curse. I remember the day Melvin was chosen. A dark cloud loomed over me as I watched him walk to the table to choose one of the Bibles. I prayed the slip of paper hidden inside would not be his. A big responsibility comes with being the chosen one. Your family, your children, every word that comes out of your mouth is scrutinized. The members don't even realize it, but they set your whole family on a pedestal, and the pressure of that status is difficult."

For the next hour, he listened to his grandfather painstakingly explain his actions and what he had done to protect both him and Emma. The old man often stopped to gather his words, looking to his wife for clarity. Once he was sure Melvin had said all he wanted, he pushed himself away from the table and walked to the window over the sink, grasping the edge of the counter. "I understand it's hard, but you have to understand how I see it. You turned your back on us. You are a man who is supposed to love and take care of your flock. The two people who needed you the most you turned your back on." He turned and leaned back on the sink and folded his arms across his chest.

Melvin's shoulders slumped. "I know."

Daniel dug his thumbs into his folded arms. "My mother, Emma, Nathan, everyone around me is trying to tell me I need to forgive you. I'm not sure how I can get past this."

Melvin shifted in his chair. "By the grace of *Gott*, we'll find a way together."

Daniel headed to the door but stopped at his grandfather's side. "It would be easy for me to say I understood, and all was forgiven, but God knows my heart. Until I can honestly say I hold no grudge against you, all I can say is thank you for explaining your side of the story, and I'll give it some thought."

Without moving from his chair, Melvin mumbled. "It's all I can ask."

Chapter 13
The Letter

In the few seconds it took him to walk to his truck, years' worth of anger started to fade away. There was something about listening to his grandparents speak of their involvement in his life that calmed his anxiety. He knew the first step to healing was forgiveness. It was more than his grandfather he needed to forgive. There were still two boys, men now, he needed to face. A part of him believed he couldn't leave the past until he met the two people who haunted him.

It took a few minutes for the engine to warm before he scanned his side mirror. There, standing to the left of his rear bumper, was the man who shared his bench during church. His hands buried deep in his pocket, and his black wool hat pulled tight on his head. Daniel switched the gear back to park and pushed the driver-side door open. Without taking his eyes off the man, he stepped out and walked his way.

"I looked for you after church. I wanted to introduce myself, and I didn't catch your name."

"Jay."

Daniel extended his hand, and it took the man a few seconds before he responded to the invitation.

"Can I give you a ride somewhere?"

"No, I wasn't sure you saw me in your rearview mirror, and I didn't want to step out in front of you."

"Where are you going?"

"Home."

Daniel nodded his head toward the house. "Here?"

"Yep, for the last thirty years."

"You live here with Melvin Shetler?"

"Born and raised right here on this farm. All except a few wild years during *Rumspringa*."

"I live in the *doddi haus* out back."

"So, you're a Shetler?"

"Jay Shetler, your uncle."

Daniel looked blankly in the face of the clean-shaven man. An older image of himself. "You're my father's brother?"

"Yes, his youngest. I was only ten when he was shunned. I don't remember too much about him. *Datt* says I resemble him. But then all of us Shetler men carry the same characteristics, much like yourself."

Daniel leaned on a fence post. "I knew there was something about you that seemed familiar; I couldn't place it."

Jay motioned his head in the direction of the house. "How'd it go up there today?"

"You knew they asked me to stay?"

"*Datt* mentioned it this morning; he prayed he could convince you to talk to him today."

"So, how much do you know?"

"I know you hold him responsible. I know about Elizabeth, or Emma, as she calls herself. And I know you tend to follow in the Shetler men's footsteps."

"What's that supposed to mean?"

"Let's say you're not the first man in this family to walk the path you're on."

"I'm not sure I follow you."

"Anger runs deep in this family, and you're not the first Shetler man to drown his sorrows in a bottle."

Daniel stood up straight. "How do you know about that?"

"Let's say there's not too much about you that I don't know."

The hairs on the back of Daniel's neck stood up as he tried to comprehend how someone he just met knew so much about him. "So, you never answered me; how do you know that about me?"

"You may think *datt* turned his back on you, but that man spent the last twenty-one years making sure you were safe, and that goes for Elizabeth as well."

Daniel looked over his shoulder at the house and then back to his uncle. "You see, the problem is, I wasn't safe at all. No matter how much he thinks he was looking out for me."

"We all face things in life that leave us broken, and it's those things that make us stronger. Your grandfather spent his life in repentance for turning his back on you, and not once did he let you out of his sight. He always knew where you were, what you were doing, and how to save you. The one time he couldn't save you from the unspeakable, he pulled you from the situation before it turned more dangerous."

Daniel stood speechless at his uncle's declaration. The chill in the air magnified as his uncle walked past him, adding, "Get over yourself before it's too late."

"Too late for what?"

Without answering, Jay walked away and it became evident, he wouldn't get an answer, Daniel climbed back in his truck.

~~

Jay sat at the small oak table staring at the same page in his Bible he'd been trying to read for the last ten minutes. The warm glow of the oil lamp bounced shadows off the words as they swirled in his head.

No matter how many times he read the passage, it wouldn't register through the task weighing on his shoulders.

Thoughts of living in the shadow of his oldest *bruder's* memory cost him a life with Mary Sue, and the magnitude of what he gave up wore a hole in his heart. She'd been patient for the first five years, but when she couldn't wait any longer, she moved on.

He closed the leather-bound Bible, folded his hands, and rested his head on his arms. Time was dwindling for his *datt,* and if he couldn't convince Daniel to take what was rightfully his, he'd lose everything he worked so hard to obtain. He walked to the window and gazed out over the dairy farm. His five older *bruder's* had businesses and families of their own. As the youngest, it was his responsibility to care for his parents and take over the farm operation. The only family member left to help him was Daniel. How was he ever going to convince the boy to own up to the responsibility he had to his family? If Daniel didn't come back into the folds of his heritage, all would be lost. He walked to the door, grabbed his hat and coat, and let the brisk air freeze the hairs in his nostrils. His nightly ritual of checking on his parents became more of a habit than a duty.

He stomped his boots off on the porch before opening the door as the comforting aroma of apple pie and coffee greeted him. His mother held her finger to her lips, requesting him to tread quietly. With every passing day, his father's health declined as he snored softly in his chair. His mother motioned him to the kitchen.

"How's he feeling today?"

"About the same."

"I saw Dr. Madden's car yesterday afternoon. What did he say?"

"It won't be long, and the visible signs of cancer will be hard to hide."

Jay pulled the chair out and sat to the right of his father's designated spot at the head of the table. "I'm running out of time."

Lillian laid a hand on his shoulder. "I have faith that *Gott* will answer our prayers. You're doing everything your father asked of you. It's all up to Daniel now."

"But if I can't get him to agree to work this farm, I fear I might lose it. I can't run an operation like this by myself."

"Now, son, your older *bruder's* will help if it comes to that, but again, I'm trusting Daniel makes the right decision."

Jay moved the sugar bowl closer to his cup and stirred in a hefty spoon into the black liquid. "He's bullheaded. Just like every other man in this family."

"You've been watching over your nephew for months now, and I'm certain you'll figure it out."

"But what if he doesn't?"

"He will, I'm sure of it."

~~

Daniel laid on his bed with his hands folded up under his head, staring off into the darkness. There was something his uncle was not telling him; he was certain of it. What did he mean, don't wait too long? He swung his legs over the edge of the bed and rested his chin in his elbows and thought. *If only I could talk to Katie, she'd help me figure it out.* He missed her cornflower blue eyes and the way the top of her *kapp* smelled like sugar cookies. He pulled the familiar, blue-lined paper from the drawer and reread her latest letter.

Daniel,

The weather still has a sharpness about it, but yet I see tiny hopes of spring everywhere I turn. I saw a Robin the other day, and the crocuses around the flower garden are starting to peek their way through the snow.

I'm happy you're finding contentment working in Nathan's stables. If you're anything like me, a hard day's work always makes me feel better.

You asked in my last letter if I truly forgave you and the answer is yes. I don't want you to think twice about it. That wasn't you, and it was a version of yourself I'm sure you're not happy with. Lord willing, if we never see that side again, it will be a good day.

As far as how I could offer you forgiveness so quickly, all I can say is this. Jesus taught us to pray. "Forgive us our trespasses as we forgive those who trespass against us." When we withhold forgiveness from others, we block the life and forgiveness Gott wants to give us. If you are still struggling with your grandfather, please remember this. We are to forgive as we have been forgiven. God has made forgiveness available to all people. To withhold that is not in our power.

I mentioned to Mamm the other day how much I miss Emma, she suggested I take a bus and visit. She said I'd need to clear it with Datt first, so I pray he will be open to the idea. Even though I do miss Emma, it's you I miss the most. Part of me feels guilty in deceiving my parents, but my thoughts are so consumed with you, I'd do almost anything to see you again."

Forever and always,
Katie

The corner of his lip curved up as he stuffed the letter back in its envelope and secured it back in the drawer. What was it about that girl, and how would he ever make it work? She was so young, and there was no way her father would willingly let her become involved with an *Englisher*. Was he English, or was he becoming more and more Amish with every passing day? Could that be the one thing that would finally put his life on the right path? So many unanswered questions.

The need to talk to Jay forced him to his feet and down the steps to the stables. Walking past the horses, he thought about the satisfaction he got from working with animals. Maybe a start would be staying in Sugarcreek. But what about Katie? It wasn't the first time that thought had crossed his mind.

Instead of heading to the truck, he moved toward the buggy shed. It might be the first step in considering turning his back on his worldly ways to embrace his Amish heritage. Offering forgiveness suddenly became his mission. Before he went to his grandfather, he needed to get to the bottom of Jay. He hooked up the buggy to the horse as déjà vu covered him much like the snow-filled lawn. In the quietness of the night, a voice much like before, whispered in his ear. *"This is the path I've chosen for you."*

He didn't need to turn around to see where the message came from. It was an understanding and an end to the bitterness he held inside. He positioned himself high on the bench of the black enclosed buggy and let the cool air clear his head to fully grasp the message he'd received from God.

The five miles to his grandfather's dairy farm gave him ample time to figure out the questions he had for his uncle. There was something about how he moved, the way he talked, and the way he seemed to know things that didn't quite sit right. Like a light bulb turning on for the first time, the random messages came to mind, and then it clicked.

"JS, Jay Shetler?" His voice bounced off the canvas walls as pieces started to fall in place. *Why and how? Somebody has some explaining to do,* he thought. He slapped the reins harder, encouraging the black mare to trot faster.

The light from the window of the *doddi haus* acted as a beacon guiding his way down the long driveway to the small cottage. He tethered the horse to the hitching post, took the steps two at a time, and pounded heavily on the front door. It opened, and Jay stood back as

136

Daniel breached the threshold. Jay waved him inside and said, "I assume by the look on your face you've figured a few things out."

Daniel didn't bother taking off his boots but closed the door and stood on the small-braided rug just inside the door.

"You might as well take your stuff off and have a seat. You'll be here a while."

Daniel slipped out of his boots as Jay pointed to the seat of the willow rocker and folded the paper he'd left on the chair. Daniel sat on the edge and asked,

"Have you been following me?"

"I wouldn't call it following. I'd call it making sure you didn't do anything stupid."

"So, how did that work out for you?"

"You tell me. All I could do was work on your conscience."

Daniel dropped his head and kept his eyes on his feet., "I guess I've done a lot of stupid things over the last few months."

"Your words, not mine."

"But why? What could you possibly gain by keeping me out of trouble?"

"I made a promise."

"A promise to who?"

Jay put his chair in motion with his foot. "It doesn't matter who, just that I did."

Daniel sat back in his chair and rested his hands on the arms. He wrapped his knuckles around the polished wood and the muscle in his jaw twitched as Jay ran in circles to his questions. "For whose benefit? What could you achieve by cleaning up my messes?"

"As I said before, I've been in your shoes."

Jay nodded his head in the direction of the main house and said, "Those two people up there have spent a lifetime trying to make things right. If I have any control of the situation, I'm not going to let history repeat itself."

"I still don't see how anything I do will affect them."

"Well, then I guess I still have some explaining to do. To start with, *Datt* has put me in charge of convincing you to run this dairy with me. He is stepping back from the day-to-day operation and is leaving it to both of us. Neither of us can run it alone, and it will take both of us to keep it going."

Jay walked to the bookshelf in the corner of the room and reached for a small tin box. Before turning to face him, he leafed through the papers. Closing the lid and placing the box back on the shelf, he turned and handed Daniel a letter.

"As far as me watching over you, maybe this will enlighten you more."

Daniel held the yellowed paper closer to the light.

Dear Bruder,

Wherever you find yourself in life, I hope these few words will set your path straight. I've left explicit instructions with Mamm to hand this letter to any, and all, that find themselves sitting on the fence to the English world. If you think the worldly ways of the English appeal to you for one minute, let me share a few things I've discovered.

Fast cars, false promises, and independence come with a price. Our parents raised us with values that will be forever lost once we leave the confines of the g'may. The minute you step one foot across those boundaries, you may never find your way back. I sit here, a mere image of the man I could have been, admitting to myself I see no way back.

The shame of being shunned is a pain I'll never forget. I've done too much, seen too many things, hurt too many people to turn back now. So, if you think your Rumspringa is full of adventure with no responsibilities, think twice. I'm married with two children to a woman who doesn't deserve the pain I've caused her. I've done things I'm ashamed of. I'll surely go to hell.

I've disgraced our family, don't do the same.
Jake

Daniel held the letter up, "My dad wrote this?"

"He did. It came the same day *Datt* bailed me out of jail. The next day we got word he'd been killed."

Chapter 14
A Change of Heart

Emma and Rachel stood at the end of the long farmhouse table in Nathan's kitchen, cutting out flowers and stars with metal cookie cutters. A winter storm whistled around the house, but the sweet smell of cookies and a warm fire made it a perfect day to stay inside.

"Look, Emma, I cut them out real close together just like you did," Rachel exclaimed.

Emma took a towel and brushed the flour off the end of Rachel's nose. "You're doing a great job. Your *datt* will enjoy these with his evening cup of coffee for sure and certain."

Rachel carefully lifted the cookies from the table and placed them on the waiting cookie sheet. "Marie, do you like what I've cut out so far?"

Marie stood at the kitchen sink washing breakfast dishes and looked over her shoulder. "I think you're doing great, and I can't wait to try one myself."

Marie buried her hands in the hot sudsy water and looked out the window overlooking Nathan's farm. A warm smile crested her lips as she thought how her heart swelled with caring for Nathan's children. It was only a few more weeks, and she'd be officially their *mamm*.

Once filled with lost hope and broken dreams, her life was now full of love and acceptance. She never dreamed she'd find a way to see God's goodness in her life, but the last eight months proved she was not only forgiven but loved. Even Emma and Daniel had let her be an active part of their lives again.

She followed the giggles to where Emma lovingly taught Rachel the ins and outs of baking. The pain of her past was becoming only a fleeting memory. She had found a way to forgive herself and earned the love of a good man, giving her purpose again. Before she had a chance to dry her hands, Amos came barreling in the kitchen and stopped short of running into her. The dark-haired five-year-old wasted no time in finding his way to the bowl of cookie dough.

"Can I have a bite, pretty please?" He begged.

Marie nodded in Emma's direction as she dropped a ball of the buttery dough in his mouth.

Marie sat at the end of the table and rested her chin in the palm of her hand. "I haven't seen Daniel in a couple of days; Nathan said he's been spending time at Melvin's. Do you know what he's doing over there?"

Emma brushed the flour from her hands and reached for the cup of tea. "I did talk to him for a few minutes last night, and he said he'd explain everything to us tonight after supper."

"I'm glad he's getting to know your father's family."

Emma walked to the stove, added water to her cup, and sat at the table next to Marie. "Lillian ask if I'd come to spend some time with her this week. She says she has some things to show me."

Emma stirred honey in her tea and swirled the spoon around until it was clean. Clanking it on the side of her mug and laying it on a napkin, she said, "I don't have any ill feelings toward either one of them. If it weren't for them, I think I would've had a much different childhood. But that's different for Daniel. I keep praying *Gott* will lay it on his heart to offer *Mommi* and *Doddi* Shetler grace."

Marie brushed crumbs off the table in a napkin. "Melvin is responsible for convincing the ministers that I was more than ready to be baptized into the church. With Nathan's standing in the community and Melvin's instruction, the *g'may* welcomed me with open arms. I never dreamed they would permit me to marry him in such a short time. Again, I owe all of that to him. There were many things over the years that he did behind the scenes that none of us ever knew. I hope and pray Daniel will come to appreciate all he did for all of us."

Emma patted the back of her mother's hand. "Mama, I'm so happy for you. This was all part of *Gott'*s plan for us."

Marie looked at her daughter and whispered, "God is good."

Marie quickly wiped a tear from the corner of her eye, stood up, and placed her hands on her hips. "Well, enough of that, we have work to do. Emma, if you and Rachel will finish these cookies and clean up the kitchen, I'll check on Rosie. Maybe she'll walk me through cutting out my wedding dress."

~~

Emma bundled up against the cold to go to *Mommi* Lillian's house. They made plans to spend the afternoon working on a quilt together. Just as she stepped foot off the *doddi haus* porch, she heard metal wheels crunch on the frozen ground behind her. She stood at the edge of the driveway and paused until it came into view. Daniel, clad in a black wool coat and felt brimmed hat, sat high on the bench. She held a hand up over her eyes to block the glare of the sun and smiled at her brother.

Daniel pulled back on the reins and made the black mare stop mere inches from where she stood. "I'm going to the livestock auction with Jay. Nathan wants me to check on what horses come up on the auction block, and Jay's checking out a lot of heifers."

Emma took a few steps closer to where Daniel sat, "Are you heading to Jay's now?"

"I am. Do you need a ride?"

"I promised Lillian I'd spend the day with her."

"Perfect timing then."

Daniel reached under the wooden bench for the wool blanket for Emma to cover her lap. When she got settled, he lifted the reins to put the buggy in motion.

The bright sun warmed Emma's face even though the open-air wagon left her exposed to the elements. She wrapped her scarf tighter around her neck before asking, "So, what's up with the clothes?"

"Even I agree Nathan's old wool coat and hat is warmer than my baseball cap and denim jacket."

"You're looking a bit Amish today." Emma secured the blanket around her legs. "It suits you."

Daniel looked around her to check for traffic before pulling out on the road. "It might suit me better than you think."

"Why's that?"

"Seems like Melvin hasn't stopped pulling strings with my life, and not only with me but with Jay as well."

Emma crinkled up her forehead and looked his way. "What does Jay have to do with it?"

"Looks like the only way he can take over Shetler Dairy is to convince me to help him run it."

"How do you feel about that?"

"One more decision about my life without me having a say in the matter."

"Do you think wanting you to help in the family business is another way of controlling your life?"

Daniel pulled back on the reins at the stop sign and looked both ways before proceeding through the intersection, and said, "I'm sure of it."

Emma weighed her words before she responded. "You still have some issues with how he handled everything, but I think you need to look at the bigger picture. As I see it, he wants to make up for some of those decisions. Asking you to take an active role at the dairy might be his way of apologizing."

"He didn't ask. He held it over Jay's head to convince me."

Daniel's voice was taut, and Emma didn't dare press him. She needed to find a way to soften his attitude toward their *doddi,* but for now, she'd let him be. Maybe *Mommi* Lillian would have an idea.

~~

Lillian pulled the pleated curtain back in the living room when she heard voices outside. Emma and Daniel had pulled up and were talking with Jay. She looked at her granddaughter, and her heart swooned, opening the door before Emma had a chance to knock.

"Come in, my dear, and hurry before you let all the heat out."

Emma took off her brown winter bonnet and slipped out of her boots.

"It was chilly riding in the open wagon."

"I can only imagine. Come to the kitchen and let me fix you a cup of my favorite hot chocolate. I have it warming on the stove and it's sure to warm you up."

Lillian poured it into the two mugs waiting on the table. "Thank you so much for coming for a visit. I have the quilt rack set up in the front room, and I'm looking forward to our little chat."

Emma looked toward the front room and asked, "Where's *Doddi* Melvin?"

"He's feeling under the weather; I persuaded him to stay in bed today."

144

"I can come back another day if he's not feeling well. I wouldn't want to keep you from tending to him."

"You'll do no such thing. I've been looking forward to this all week."

Lillian held up her hand and said, "Wait," just as Emma started to take a sip.

"I didn't stir in my secret ingredient yet." Emma pushed the cup back to her.

Lillian picked up a small glass jar off the center of the table and held it close as she took the cover off. She breathed in the contents. "Ahhh, I love this."

A whiff of vanilla and chocolate filled the air. "Vanilla powder?" Emma asked.

A smile added more creases to her grandmother's face, and she held her finger up to her lips. "Shhh...now if I tell you, you have to promise to keep it a secret. I've never told anyone what makes my hot chocolate so special. I'm getting up there in years, and it's time to pass it on."

With no daughters of her own, sharing her secret ingredient with her eldest granddaughter touched her. She whispered, "White chocolate shavings." She stirred a heaping spoonful in Emma's cup. "I hope you find a way to keep my secret safe until a time like this when you find that one person to pass it on to."

Emma picked up her cup and brought it to her nose. "Thank you so much for entrusting me with it. I promise to guard it with my life until the time is right."

Lillian took off the cover of the cake pan in front of her. "I made pound cake this morning. Would you like some?"

In a yearning tone, Emma answered, "Pound cake was my *mamm's* favorite."

"I'm sorry, dear, I'm sure you miss her."

145

Emma took a bite of the buttery cake. "It was *Gott's* will, and I'm happy I got to spend as much time with her as I did."

Lillian added a slice to the plate in front of her. "Your Aunt Anna Mae told me a lot about Stella. I wish I could have met her."

With a crack in her voice, Emma said. "I still can't believe she's gone. I try not to speak of her much around Marie. But I do miss talking about her."

Emma wrapped both hands around her cup and rested her elbows on the table. "I'm afraid I'll forget things about her if I don't force myself to remember her often. "

Lillian reached across the table and laid her hand on Emma's forearm. "You can consider this your safe zone. You go right ahead and talk about your *mamm,* as much as you want."

"You have no idea what that means to me. Thank you, Lillian."

"Please, call me *Mommi.* I may not have been around when you were little, but if you'll let me, we'll make up for lost time."

A noise from the other room pulled Lillian's attention away from the table and forced her to follow the sound. "I'll be right back."

Emma skimmed the row of medicine bottles on the Lazy-Susan in the middle of the table. Her stomach flipped with the sight of Melvin's name printed clearly across each one. She examined one of the prescriptions, recalling the same medicine her *mamm* had taken.

"He won't take most of those," her *Mommi's* voice sounded behind her.

Emma turned to face her, still holding the pill bottle in her hand. "What's the matter with him?"

Lillian took a chair and dropped her shoulders before responding. "He doesn't want anyone to know."

"Know what?"

"About his cancer."

146

Emma's posture folded beside her at the table. "No, it can't be, not cancer."

"I'm afraid so, but you have to promise to keep it to yourself. "

"Does Daniel know? "

"Especially Daniel, you can't breathe a word. Your *doddi* doesn't want to add pressure to the boy."

"Does this have anything to do with him working the farm, and why doesn't he want him to know?"

Lillian paused and folded her hands on her lap. "It's a long story, but I think his issue is he wants Daniel to come back into the folds of the family on his own. He's afraid if he told him about his health, he'll agree out of guilt or obligation."

Emma watched worry lines fill *Mommi* Lillian's face. "So, what is the doctor saying?"

"Nothing else can be done, and before long, what he's tried to hide all these months will become obvious."

An ache filled Emma's chest with the thought of having to face another family member dying. How could she keep this from Daniel? "I think we should tell him. It's what he needs to hear, that *Doddi* Melvin and Jay need his help."

"Melvin is a proud man, and he's put everything in place so that Jay can carry on with the dairy farm. At this point, it's all in God's hands. Nothing I can say will change his mind. I learned over the years that it's my place to be supportive, but his to decide what's best for this family."

Emma wished she could find the words to convince her *Mommi* Lillian they should be honest with Daniel. Another secret would only make things worse, but she could tell she was adamant about letting Melvin handle things in his own manner.

Lillian headed to the front room. "Come on, let's get to work. Many a problem can be solved between the stitches and thread of a new quilt."

Emma followed Lillian and tucked a chair under the rainbow of colors stretched between the rack. She picked up the needle and thread and started to weave tiny little stitches in the quilt top. Both she and Lillian found a rhythm of rocking the needle back and forth, making hundreds of tiny stitches in a flowery pattern.

Emma stopped to thread her needle. "This broken star pattern is beautiful. Is it for someone special?"

Lillian peered over her wire-rim glasses sitting low on her nose, and the corner of her mouth turned into a mischievous smile. "Do the colors appeal to you?"

"Oh yes, the shades of purple are beautiful."

"Perfect, because it belongs to you."

All at once, Emma's nose twitched, and emotion welled up inside. "The purples remind me of the purple and white pansies I used to plant along my *mamm's* picket fence. She loved flowers."

"What a sweet memory. When my own *mamm* died, I couldn't look at a rose bush without thinking of her. To this day, roses will send me down memory lane."

Lillian had a far-away look on her face. "I believe the Lord gives us the beauty of nature to remind us of His glory on our darkest days."

Emma smiled at her grandmother's comment and thought about how much she was enjoying getting to know her.

~~

Daniel found his seat next to his uncle at the Sugarcreek Auction House. The half-moon-shaped arena was filling with a mixture of wide-brimmed black hats and blue jeans. Daniel popped the top on a soda can and took a chug before setting it on the floor between his feet and turned toward Jay.

"It looks like the heifer sale is first."

Jay studied the flyer he grabbed on the way up the steps and read through the auction items. "The first lot of fifteen is what I have my eye on. I checked outback, and they are healthy. This is the first step in expanding our herd this year. "

Jay pushed his bangs back under the brim of his hat. "Have you given any more thought to *Datt's* offer to work the farm with me?"

"I've been English my whole life, not so sure acknowledging my birthright now sits well with me."

"Like I told you before, once a Shetler, always a Shetler, and it doesn't matter what you call yourself."

"That's what you keep saying, but I have ties to Willow Springs."

"Your ties are here and this farm."

A flicker of irritation crept up the back of Daniel's neck as he contemplated his grandfather's offer.

Jay kept one eye on the arena and flipped his auction card up when the auctioneer sang out the price. Without missing a beat, he asked, "What hold does Willow Springs have on you? Your adopted parents or a special friend?"

"It doesn't matter who, just that it does," Daniel replied.

Jay circled a few items on the auction flyer and said, "Spend some time with him, and you'll see he's not trying to control you. He's trying to make up for lost time."

Over the last couple of days, the heaviness in Daniel's chest started to lighten. Even that morning, when he borrowed Nathan's hat and wool jacket, it was like a light bulb went off. Maybe Jay was right; perhaps it was time he quit looking back and started concentrating on what was in front of him instead.

~~

Melvin sat in the rocker near the bedroom window he'd shared with Lillian for the past fifty years. Somewhere deep inside, he knew his time was growing short, and he prayed he'd find a way to convince Daniel to come home. If only *Gott* would grant him this one last request. With each passing day, the strength he once had to lead his family and community faded away. He rested his head on the back of the cane willow rocker, closed his eyes, and prayed.

Our Father, who art in heaven, hallowed be thy name; thy kingdom come; thy will be done on earth as it is in heaven. Give us this day our daily bread and forgive us our trespasses as we forgive those who trespass against us; and lead us not into temptation but deliver us from evil. For thy is the power and glory forever. Amen

When words didn't come to mind, that simple prayer gave him peace. He laid the Bible on the stand and shuffled the three steps to bed. He sat on the edge and pulled his pajama bottoms' fabric to lift his legs to the mattress. He looked back at his favorite chair, and something told him he wouldn't have too many more days to enjoy it.

Chapter 15
Relapse

Daniel nodded his head in the direction of the snack bar. "Do you want anything?"

Jay tapped the end of the pencil on the auction card and shook his head from side to side. The arena continued to fill as the afternoon horse auction was about to begin. Daniel weaved his way between the blue and black-clad spectators to the top of the auction house. The line at the snack bar edged the back wall as groups of men followed the aroma of hot pretzels and popcorn.

From somewhere behind him, a deep laugh stopped him in his tracks. His throat tightened, and his fist instantly clenched. The blank stare he met the cashier with left her asking if he was alright. After paying, he followed the u-shaped counter to the opposite wall and turned to study the men's faces in line. Even though eleven years had passed, the man who stood mere feet from him made the hair on his arms stand to attention. Oblivious to Daniels' recognition, the man walked past and disappeared into the crowd.

The smell of the popcorn he held in his hand suddenly turned his stomach, and he dropped it in the trash. The cold drink relaxed his throat while he scanned the room. The light brown work coat matched some of the surrounding English men, so he singled him out by size. Across the room, perched on the top bench, the greasy baseball cap and stained jacket forced his mind to remember the stench of the red and white handkerchief they used to gag his screams.

Without taking his eyes off the figure, he zigzagged his way back to Jay.

"There you are, they're about to start." Jay handed him the flyer for the retired racehorses on the docket. "You'll need to look these over quickly."

Jay elbowed him. "Did you hear me?"

Daniel glanced over the flyer before turning his attention to the auctioneer. The instructions Nathan gave him about the horses swirled around his head, clouded by the image of his past. Without saying a word, he dropped the flyer to the floor and climbed the steps toward the door.

By the time he got to the back of the building and out the double doors, the cold air did little to cool the heat rising to his face. Taking the steps two at a time, he headed to the wagon, untethered the horse, and threw the reins up over its back. The horse responded to the click of his tongue, moving the wagon away from the surrounding buggies.

Without giving any thought to Jay or the horses, he pulled out into the street and headed home. He encouraged the horse to trot faster as he weaved in and out of the side streets of Sugarcreek until he found his way back to the highway. The urgency to go to his truck left any sense of logic fluttering in the wind behind him. The familiar man's voice pounded heavily in his ears, and even the constant clip-clop of the metal-lined hooves on the black pavement didn't drown the noise. Back at Nathan's, he pulled the wagon in an open-air structure, unhitched the horse, and headed straight for the familiar black Ford.

"Daniel?" Marie's voice carried in the wind with a sense of concern.

He heard his name as he climbed inside. Ignoring the sound his tires made on the ice, he passed his mother without acknowledging her call.

He kept his eyes glued to the driveway and toward the road, anxious to be set free once again.

~~

The screen door behind Marie slammed, and Nathan rested his hand in the small of her back.

"Where's he going in such a hurry?"

"I'm not sure. I called out to him, but he acted as if he didn't hear me. He pulled that wagon into the barn so fast I thought for sure something was the matter."

Nathan stepped closer and wrapped his arm around her shoulder. "I sent him to the auction this morning to bid on a couple of horses. Certainly, it's not ended yet."

"Wherever he was going, he's in a mighty hurry," Marie said, crossing her arms over her chest and rubbing them. "Too cold out here for me."

Nathan reached back to open the door and followed her back inside.

Marie walked to the treadle sewing machine in the corner of the living room and sat down and picked up the cornflower blue fabric spread out in front of her.

Nathan stood behind her and tugged at the black lacy veil she wore. Marie turned her head and looked up and smiled at her future husband.

"It won't be long, and you'll be replacing this with something more fitting of your new life."

The way he smiled back at her made her pulse quicken. "That I will."

She shooed him away with the back of her hand. "Go, I have work to do."

His broad shoulders swayed toward the door, and she thought. *Only a few more days and my life will be complete.* She couldn't help but

153

think everything she'd been through was God's way of leading her to that exact moment in time. One more thing concerned her, and that was the unsettling look in Daniel's eyes.

~~

Daniel pulled into the convenience store and wasted no time in finding relief the only way he knew how. The pull tab hissed and the muscles in his jaw relaxed as he swirled the malty liquid over his tongue. He downed the first can before pulling back out to the highway. He went straight back to the auction house and parked on the side of the cement block building, popped another tab and then another and another. The rage consuming his thoughts turned into blurred chaos. Even leaving Jay to fend for himself, he felt no remorse.

After two hours, the man's figure appeared a few yards from where he waited, and he slithered down in the seat when he passed. Lifting his head high enough to look in the side rearview mirror, the man disappeared behind the building. Weight in his chest pounded, and he stepped out into the parking lot. He stumbled before pulling himself up on the side of the white building and picked up his pace. As he rounded the corner, he hollered. "You!" The stout man stopped and turned in his direction.

Adrenaline gave him an edge of courage, and he quickened his steps toward the dark-haired figure.

Slurring his words. "We have so...me, " he closed his eyes as if the words were too challenging to sputter out, he finally managed to croak out, "unfinished bus....iness to take care of."

A gruff voice responded, "You're drunk, and I'm not looking for any trouble."

Daniel swayed to the left, and struggled to say, "You might not be look....ing for it bu....t you got it."

In an instant, he lunged toward the man knocking him up against the white wall. The man pushed back, sending Daniel across the ice-covered gravel. Finding his way back to his feet, he flailed his arms, connecting with the cinder block wall. He fell to his knees, clenching his fist to his stomach and the man dug his dirty boot into his rib cage and then the side of his face.

The pain left him gasping for air. He dropped his head on the cold ground and closed his eyes as the man's deep voice echoed through the air. "Once a scrawny kid, always a scrawny kid."

~~

Jay caught a glimpse of Daniel's truck as his neighbor pulled into the street. "Stop, he must've come back for me. Thanks for offering me a ride anyway."

Jay climbed down from the enclosed black buggy and walked toward the side of the building. An empty beer can on the ground made him hiss under his breath. He followed the footprints to the red splattered snow that gave way to his nephew, face buried in the frozen ground.

He knelt beside him and turned him over pushing his finger up under his jawbone. When a steady pulse bounced off his fingertip, he scanned the rest of his body. Besides the gashes on his knuckles and cheek, there were no outward signs of serious injuries. In one swift movement, he swung him over his shoulder, much like the bags of feed he was so accustomed to hauling. With little thought to Daniel's comfort, he opened the tailgate and laid him on the cold metal. He slammed it shut, crawled into the driver's side, and threw his hat on the seat. The last thing he needed was for one of the ministers to catch him driving.

His short hop over the fence during *Rumspringa* yielded him a driver's license, which came in handy when it came to making sure his late *bruder's* son stayed out of trouble. His shoulders tensed as he counted five empty cans on the floorboard. He fought the urge to drop Daniel off in front of the police station instead of taking him back to Bouteright Stables.

He slowly pulled up beside Nathan's office door at the stables. Only after he turned the engine off did he push the hair off his forehead and put his hat back on. The minute he opened the door, Nathan walked outside, flipping his jacket upon his shoulders. "Problem?"

"*Jah*, I'd say we have a problem." Jay walked to the back of the truck.

"What on earth did he get into this time?" Nathan asked.

"Not sure; I found him like this."

Nathan fastened his coat closed. "He raced outta here a couple of hours ago like something was on fire."

"Well, he left me stranded at the auction in about the same manner."

"As much as I could tell, his fist met the wall of the auction house."

Jay opened the tailgate and shook his head. "I thought I was getting through to him."

Nathan moved closer. "Is that beer I smell?"

"A six-pack as far as I can tell."

Nathan walked to the side of the building and filled a metal bucket at the spigot. It only took him two long strides before throwing the ice-cold water on Daniel's chest.

The shock forced Daniel to heave. He wiped his mouth on the back of his sleeve and tried to push himself up, but the sharp pain made him fall face first back in his mess. He rolled on his back, moaned, and pulled himself up with the other hand.

It didn't take but a minute for Daniel to register the faces staring back at him. Nathan and Jay stood with solemn looks, and not far behind stood Marie. She didn't say a word but turned and walked away. Nathan headed back to his office and said, "Boy, you're on the road to destruction. You better find a way to get your act together, or you're going to end up just like your father."

Jay let Nathan finish before he added, "You're on your own from here on. I've said and done all I can do."

~~

There wasn't a part of Daniel's body that wasn't frozen. The last couple of hours were a blur in his mind, but the disappointment in the faces he witnessed sobered him up faster than the bucket of water. He left his truck parked and walked around to the outside entrance of the loft above. A hot shower in the stable bathroom would help clear his head. He sat down on the edge of the bed and kicked off his boots. A handwritten note from his mother lay next to the windup clock on the nightstand.

Daniel,
This letter came for you last week, but it got mixed in a couple of feed catalogs. I found it this morning while cleaning off the counter, but you had already left.
Mama

Katie's familiar handwriting was a breath of fresh air, but he left it where it lay until he showered. He needed to wash away so many things before he could hear her voice through the lines on the paper.

His pulse raced as he showered. In the past, every time he remembered the beady eyes and yellowed teeth of his past, revenge

157

boiled up inside of him. At that moment, something snapped, and the pain in his mother's eyes bore a hole in his heart. Did Nathan really think he'd end up like his father, and what did Jay mean he was on his own? Had he ruined his chance of taking his rightful place beside him at Shetler Dairy?

He let the hot water beat on his back and called out to God. *"Please forgive me; I've made a mess of things once again. If you want me to forgive, you'll need to put it on my heart because you know it's hard. I don't want to be angry anymore. More than anything, I don't want to end up like my father."*

There was something that swirled down the drain that gave him a sense of peace. All of a sudden, he knew what he needed to do. He never understood the freedom of forgiving more than he did at that very moment. After dressing, he sat in the chair at the edge of his bed and pulled his boots back on; Katie's letter was like a beacon of hope waiting to be read. He stood near the window and held her words to the light.

Daniel,

I've convinced my parents to let me come and visit Emma. I've put a few dollars away from my baking and had enough to buy a bus ticket to Sugarcreek. I'll arrive on Monday at 6 PM. I hope you're able to meet me.

Forever and always, Katie

Daniel peeked at the clock; it was five. He had just enough time to get across town to the bus station. Stopping at the back of his truck, the smell of stale beer forced him to hook up the hose and spray it away. Shame lingered on his dry lips as he washed the remnants of the afternoon away. He filled the metal bucket with emptied beer cans from the floorboard and dumped them in the trash. There was no sense in hiding what he did, and he was sure it wouldn't be the last he'd hear of it. The clang of the aluminum against the bucket pierced his ears as he tried to push away the disgrace he held for himself.

He turned the key and the roar of the engine, which any other time brought him joy, left a hollow pit deep in his stomach. He turned the key off and patted the dashboard. "Goodbye, girl, we've been through a lot together, but it's time."

With that, he walked back to the barn and hitched up one of the black enclosed buggies.

***

Katie picked up the small black bag at her feet and rested it on her lap to anticipate the next stop. For the last three hours, she sat in the front seat of the Greyhound bus marveling at everything they passed. She'd only been away from Willow Creek one other time, and that was to visit her *datt's schwester* in Indiana. While she was excited to see Emma, the butterflies in her stomach only flew for Daniel.

She was sure her parents would have never allowed her to come had they known the real condition of her heart. The bus driver announced their arrival in Sugarcreek, and she scanned the parking lot looking for Daniel. Waiting for the woman next to her to exit, she made her way down the steps and onto the waiting platform. A nervousness that he might not come for her was short-lived when she heard her name.

"Katie, over here."

The smile on her lips was hard to hide as she followed his voice. He took her bag from her hand and pulled her close. Embarrassed by his public show of affection, she pulled away slightly before he squeezed her tighter.

Daniel sucked in a deep breath through his nose and said, "Yep, that's my Katie, still smells like sugar cookies."

"Sugar cookies?" she whispered in a slight giggle.

He rested his chin on the top of her head. "Yep, sugar cookies."

Katie pushed herself away and looked into his eyes. "I've missed you."

He took her hand and led her away from the bus platform. "So, Emma has no idea you're here?"

"Nope, I wanted to surprise her."

"She'll be ecstatic, I'm sure. How long are you staying?"

"Two weeks." Daniel's grin reached ear to ear, and there was no denying he was happy with her answer.

"That gives us plenty of time."

"Plenty of time for what?" She asked.

"For whatever your heart desires."

Katie leaned in closer and whispered, "You."

Daniel winked and squeezed her hand.

When he guided her to the waiting buggy, she asked, "Where's your truck?"

"One of the many things we need to talk about."

Katie let him help her up in the canvas-lined buggy and said, "I was quite looking forward to the warmth of your truck."

"Well, you might as well get that notion out of your head. I'm afraid old Betsy girl's seen the last of Daniel Miller."

Katie tipped up her head and waited for an explanation. Daniel snapped the canvas shut and hollered as he made it around to his side of the buggy. "Let's say God showed me things I needed to see today."

Questions were swirling around in Katie's head, and before she was able to put them in any sense of order, he continued.

"I disappointed quite a few people today, but I'm not going to make the same mistake twice."

Katie pointed to the gashes on his knuckles and face. "Oh my, what did you do?"

"Trust me when I say I had to learn a lesson the hard way."

Katie sensed the remorse in his tone and felt it better she didn't press him. If it was something he wanted to share, he'd tell her in his own time. For now, she'd enjoy sitting next to him and treasure every moment of the next fourteen days.

"So, anything specific you want to do while you're here?" He asked.

"I hadn't given it any thought. Got any ideas?"

"I think what I have to figure out the most is how to share you with Emma."

Katie blushed. "I'm sure that won't be too hard. Emma's not stupid. She'll know exactly why I came."

"Now I thought you girls kept things like this a secret."

"We do, but without any sisters of my own, Emma reads me like a book."

Daniel pulled to the back of the parking lot and stopped. He reached over and pulled her close, warming her lips with his. Before pulling away, he whispered, "Does she know everything?"

"Not everything."

His breath, fresh from the mint he was sucking on, intertwined with hers as he said, "Good."

Daniel pulled the buggy back out into traffic, and Katie tried to calm the flutters of her racing pulse. She had just arrived, and she was already dreading having to return home. His warm welcome was more than she dreamed of, and she yearned for the next time his lips met hers.

Chapter 16
Katie's Visit

Katie and Emma sat at Marie's table, carefully icing the sugar cookies they made for Thursday's wedding.

"I'm so excited you're here. I can't believe you kept it a secret from me. When I saw you pull up with Daniel, I thought I was dreaming. How did you ever convince your parents to let you come for a visit?"

Katie grinned as she handed Emma the bowl of royal icing. "They knew how much I missed you, and when I offered to pay for the bus ticket myself, they couldn't say no."

Filling the piping bag, Emma outlined the tulip shaped cookie. "You can't fool me, Katie Yoder, you might've told your parents you were coming to see me, but I'm sure your eyes are on Daniel."

Katie's cheeks turned a rosy hue. "I was surprised when he picked me up in a buggy. I haven't had a chance to ask him about it. What's that about?"

Emma peered over Katie's shoulder in the front room where Marie sat reading Amos a book. She leaned in closer and whispered. "He had a rough day at the auction. I didn't get the whole story yet, but I have a feeling whatever happened has him on the fence about which direction he wants to go in life."

"What do you mean? What direction?"

"Has he told you anything about our Uncle Jay?"

"In one of his letters, he mentioned something about him wanting him to work on the dairy farm. But he didn't go into too much detail. I have so many questions, and he had some things he wants to talk to me about, but we haven't had time yet."

Emma wiped her hands on the towel that hung over her shoulder. "As soon as we get Marie and Nathan's wedding taking care of, maybe you'll have some time to spend with him."

"I'm sure of it, but I'm happy I can be here to help you and Marie."

The side door banged shut as Rachel came in, kicking off her boots and dropping her lunch box before heading to the table. "Cookies? Emma, you didn't wait for me. You promised we could do them together."

"There's plenty to do. Take care of your lunchbox and wash your hands and you can help."

Rachel busied herself at the sink and continued to chatter. "I told all of my friends at school that *Datt* and Marie were getting married on Thursday. I don't have to go to school and Marie made me a new dress. It's the same color as hers. Did you see it? It's pretty blue just like my eyes."

"I did and she did a good job on it."

Rachel climbed up on the bench and took a bite of cookie. "Yum!"

Marie walked in from the living room. "Thank you for helping me with these cookies. They'll be perfect at each place setting. I couldn't have made them all myself. Katie, you came at the exact time for a visit. Emma told me what a great baker you are. We were talking the other day about your plans for Katie's Bakery."

Katie looked at Emma and corrected Marie. "It's Katie and Emma's Sweet Shoppe. That is if I can convince her to come home."

Marie moved closer to the table to watch the girls. "Emma, maybe it's time you go home. I love having you here, but if you and Katie have plans to open the bakery, you should go home."

"I'm sure Katie can find somebody else to help her run it, and besides, I'm not so sure Rebecca's ready for me to come home just yet."

Katie moved the cookies around on the table. "You can always stay with me. I'm sure *Mamm* won't mind."

"*Datt* would be heartsick if I came back to Willow Springs and didn't come home. I don't know what to do about Rebecca." Emma looked towards Katie. "Have you talked to her?"

"I saw her at church last Sunday, and she seemed fine. Then again, I never had any problems with her. Her snappiness only comes out when you're around."

"My point exactly. For some reason she blames me for *Mamm*. There was nothing I could do. She told Anna the stress of me leaving made her sicker."

Marie wrapped her arm around Emma's shoulder and pulled her into a side hug. "Rebecca is hurting, and she needs to blame somebody, and unfortunately, that somebody is you."

Emma rearranged cookies on the tray in front of her. "I want nothing more than to come home and run that bakery with you. But if it means it'll put more stress on my family, I'm not so sure. Besides, I don't want ...never mind." Emma hesitated as if she was going to say something else, then changed her mind.

Emma stayed quiet as Marie and Katie talked about all the plans for the wedding. Even though she enjoyed spending time with Marie and the *kinner,* there was a big part of her that missed Willow Springs. Was it Rebecca that was keeping her from going home? If she was honest with herself, which she was finding more and more challenging to do, she knew she was staying away, so she didn't see the hurt in Samuel's eyes.

She was dying to ask Katie about him but didn't want to give her the wrong idea. Was she having second thoughts about putting Samuel on hold? She was afraid if she went home, she'd make it even harder for him to get on with his life. In all fairness, how could she ask him to put his life on hold while she made sense of her own?

"Emma, did you hear me?"

"I'm sorry, were you talking to me?"

Katie carried the tray of cookies to the counter. "I was, I asked if you wanted to go for a walk after the cookies are done."

Emma looked toward the window. "The sun started to come out. I think a walk sounds wonderful."

Rachel slid off the bench and ran to Marie. "Can I go too?"

Marie patted the top of the girls *kapp* covered head. "How about you let Emma and Katie go by themselves. I'm sure they have lots of catching up to do, and I've been keeping them busy the last couple of days. You can help me start supper, and besides, we promised your *datt* you'd make his favorite honey topped biscuits."

***

The bluebird sky and bright sunshine were precisely what Emma needed. Since Katie showed up, thoughts of Samuel swirled around as if he was standing in front of her.

Emma pointed to the stables. "Do you want to see the horses?

Katie skipped down the steps behind her. "Oh yes, I'd love that."

The two girls kept in perfect step with each other as they had done for the last sixteen years. Two peas in a pod, their parents would call them.

Emma tucked her arm in the crook of Katie's. "I wanna hear all about home. Have the Fisher *schwesters* played matchmaker with anyone lately? What about the Kaufman boys? The last I heard, they got caught shooting pigeons off the covered bridge and left holes in the roof." Emma's voice softened. "How about Samuel, is his shoulder giving him any more trouble?"

Katie patted her friend's hand. "You don't want to know who Teena and Lizzie Fisher are working on, do you?"

"I do. I want to hear all about it."

"No, believe me, you don't. Do you remember who their neighbor is?"

Emma dropped her head. "Oh....the Graber's."

"Yes, old man Graber is set on marrying Edna off, and word has it he's put those two old spinsters to work on Samuel. I don't think you want to hear about everything. They've been working pretty hard on Samuel, and even though he won't talk about it, I see how he is with her. He's not warmed up totally to Edna Graber yet."

Emma shuffled her feet and dropped her head. "He has every right to see whomever he wants, but between you and me, my heart is empty."

"Why don't you talk to him? He'll wait until you sort things out, I'm certain of it."

Emma stepped over a slushy pile of snow. "How can I ask him to wait when I have no idea what the future holds."

"I know you'll do what's best for you, no matter what you decide."

The girls walked across the yard and headed to where Daniel was working a horse in the enclosed corral. Katie propped her arms upon the fence railing. "Wow, I had no idea he could do that. That horse is responding to his every command."

"Yeah, I heard Nathan say that he's a natural with horses."

"He certainly acts like he's been doing it his whole life." Katie whispered, "He's looking quite dapper in that black hat and suspenders. Makes my heart do a little dance watching him."

Emma clicked her tongue a few times and shook her finger in Katie's direction. "You've got it bad for my *bruder*. I notice how his eyes sparkle when he talks about you, and you're glowing."

Katie smiled and shrugged her shoulders. She was quite forward in explaining her feelings for Daniel, but they shared very few secrets. At that very moment, she was having a hard time pulling her gaze away from the man who captured her heart. The hopelessness about them being from two different cultures melted as he pranced around the pasture dressed in plain clothes.

Emma elbowed her friend, "So what do you think of Sugarcreek?"

"That's a strange question. I haven't gotten a chance to see too much of it. Why do you ask?"

"You do realize if Daniel decides to help at the dairy, he'll stay right here."

"It crossed my mind, along with what does that do for my bakery business."

"I suppose if it's *Gott's* will that I follow Daniel to Sugarcreek, so be it. I'm sure people love baked goods here as much as they do at home."

"You know what's going to happen?"

"No, what's that?" Katie asked.

"I'll go back to Willow Springs, and you'll end up moving to Sugarcreek."

Katie giggled. "I guess we'll follow our hearts and see what *Gott* has planned."

~~

Daniel watched the girls out of the corner of his eye, unhooked the horses' halter, slapped his corner hind, and let him run. He beat the dust off his hat on his thigh and swaggered toward the girls.

"I see I have an audience. Did you enjoy the show?"

In an upbeat tone, Katie replied, "Certainly did; I had no idea you were so good with horses."

Daniel leaned on the fence in front of her. "I'd say there are lots of things you don't know about me." He winked and turned in Emma's direction. "How are the wedding plans coming?"

"I think we're about ready. I can't think of one more thing we need to do before Thursday morning. The church wagon is coming tomorrow, and we'll need your help setting up the tables. But other than that, Momma is beaming from ear to ear, which I love seeing."

Daniel propped one leg up on the fence rail. "I'm sure she's enjoying us being here. I upset her the other day, and I've been avoiding her, but I agree it's great to see her happy at last."

Emma raised an eyebrow. "You need to go talk to her."

Daniel tapped the mud off the toe of his boot. "I will. I've already apologized to Nathan, and he said the same thing. He expects me to talk to her too."

He shifted his weight to the other foot. "Do you think I can tug Katie away from you long enough to show her around?"

Katie beamed. "I'd love that. When?"

"How about tonight? If you don't already have plans."

Katie looked to Emma for her approval.

Before she had a chance to answer, Emma tugged on her arm, pulling her away from the fence. "You can have her tonight, but right now, she promised to take a walk with me."

Katie waved over her shoulder. "After supper?"

"Dress warm," he hollered back.

Emma tugged on her arm. "Come on, starry eyes, get your head out of the clouds and let's enjoy our walk."

Both girls walked in silence until they reached the road. Emma's heart warmed at the way Katie looked at Daniel, and a part of her longed for the warm way Samuel used to look at her. With each passing day, she regretted turning her back on things. Maybe, just maybe, it was time, or was it too late to repair the damage she'd done? Her biggest fear was Samuel may already have feelings for Edna.

Katie bumped into her, bringing her out of her daydream. "What are you thinking so hard about?"

"A zillion things are going through my head; home, Samuel, *Datt*, Rebecca, but most of all, how much I miss *Mamm*."

Katie locked her hand in Emma's arm. "What would she be telling you right now?"

Emma was quick to answer. "She'd be telling me to stop trying to write my own story and that *Gott* had each page already written. And all I have to do is to wait on Him to turn the page."

"I think its great advice and if you don't mind, I think I'm going to borrow it. I've been trying to figure out so many things myself. He'll bring a solution to all things in His own time, not mine. My *mamm* always says, "Quit focusing on where you're going and find the blessing in where you're at."

"Wow, I love that too, and she's right. I need to stop worrying about tomorrow and enjoy today because He's brought many blessings in my life I've totally ignored."

"Me too," Katie replied.

They walked a few hundred feet before Emma asked, "Do you think Samuel is in love with Edna?"

Katie snickered. "Heavens no! He tolerates her, at best. Do I think she's in love with him? I think she's in love with the idea of marriage, but she hasn't known him long enough to be in love. I think he only agreed to take her home after she faked a sprained ankle. He felt sorry for her and told her he'd give her a ride. More than that, I think he was trying to make you jealous. He only has eyes for you. He's been in love with you since we were kids, and everyone knows it."

"I hope you're right."

"I wouldn't wait too long to go back and tell him how you feel. If Edna's family has anything to say about it, they're already planning a fall wedding."

"Regardless of what happens with Samuel, I think it's time I go home. I need to fix things with Rebecca, and besides, the strawberry stand will open soon, and we have a bakery to run."

"Oh, Emma, that makes me happy."

Chapter 17

Grace

Marie was up before dawn, sitting at the small table in the kitchen of the *doddi haus*. She took the last sip of her now cold coffee, carried the cup to the sink, and stood at the window overlooking the garden. For the previous nine months, she called the small cottage home. Soon Emma and Daniel would help her move her things into the main house. Nathan had made it known more than once how excited he was that she agreed to become his *fraa*. Rachel and Amos accepted her position as their new *mamm*, and even Rosie, Nathan's mother, was anxious for her to become a permanent figure in their home.

She never dreamed she'd marry again, and to an Amish man at that. Her Mennonite upbringing and acceptance into the Sugarcreek community made it very easy for her to fall into her new role. She glowed as she thought of how Nathan was even hinting at having *kinner* of their own. While she certainly never dreamed of having any more children, the prospect of sharing a child with Nathan left her hopeful. She had done so many things wrong with Emma and Daniel; this was her chance to make things right with Rachel and Amos, and possibly even with more children.

The sun was starting to creep up over the horizon, leaving the sky a rosy hue. There was only one more thing she wanted to take care of before she headed to the house to make breakfast, and that was to speak to Daniel. Taking a shawl off the peg by the back door, she wrapped it around her shoulders and moved toward the stables. The crisp spring air brushed against her face, and she marveled at the crocuses pushing their way up through the ground. The budding flowers reminded her how her life was getting a fresh new start.

The stable hands were stirring, and she glanced around looking for him; when she didn't see his familiar form, she headed to the loft. Just outside his door, she tapped her fingertips on the wood.

"Come in," his voice sounded from the other side.

Marie pushed the door open and walked closer to where he sat on the edge of the bed, pulling on his boots.

"Mom, what are you doing up here? Shouldn't you be getting ready for your big day?"

"I'm heading to the house to make breakfast in a few minutes, but I wanted to talk to you first."

The way he turned his head and looked up over his eyebrows, she knew he understood what she wanted to discuss. "I want to talk about the other day."

"Yeah, about that, I haven't had a chance to explain to you what happened. I'm not so sure you want to hear what I have to say."

Marie sat on the edge of the bed. "I'm all ears. I hope you have an explanation for the condition you were in. I have to admit, when I saw you, it was a vision of your father and it wasn't a memory I enjoyed."

"Unfortunately, like my father, I've been spending time trying to escape my past."

Marie folded her hands on her lap and waited for him to continue. There wasn't anything she could say that he didn't already know, and even though she tried to hide her disappointment, she was confident he could see right through her.

He cleared his throat and began. "There's no excuse for my behavior. The only way I can explain is to let you in on a few things I've kept from you."

Daniel walked to the window and buried his hands deep in his pockets without turning to face her. He couldn't bear the pain it was going to cause.

"For years, I had nightmares of a baby crying. Those dreams would leave me anxious about not being able to help Elizabeth. It wasn't until I found Emma that they stopped. However, it wasn't long until a different memory took its place."

Daniel took a deep breath and braced himself to recall a time in his life he unsuccessfully blocked out. "I spent five years being juggled from one foster home to another. In the last house I was in, I shared a room with two teenage boys. One of those boys I came in contact with the other day at the auction."

He stood still and let out a long sigh as he stared out the window. "His face, his voice, even his smell etched itself into every part of my being. For six months, they did things to me no young boy should ever experience."

Marie's heart pounded in her chest, and she gasped for air. "Oh my. Who else knows of this?"

Daniel walked back to the bed, sat beside her, and leaned his elbows on his knees while wrenching his hands. "Only my adoptive parents and Melvin. Ever since I found out he was my grandfather, that memory surfaced again."

He paused to let what he shared settle in before he continued. "When I realized he could have saved me from that abuse, anger started to boil inside of me. The only way I could alleviate the hostility was to drown it. I'm starting to grasp the alcohol only dulls the pain, and the only way I'm going to get past it is to forgive those that I feel have wronged me. I've done things I'm ashamed of. To the point, I even hurt Katie."

Sadness filled Marie, and she tried to hide her concern, but a gasp escaped her lips.

"It's okay; Katie has forgiven me. But I need to have a conversation with Melvin, and that won't be easy, but I'm praying God will give me the words. I also know I need to forgive those two boys. Only then will I be free from it."

Marie pulled a tissue from her pocket. "Can you ever forgive me?"

"Forgive you for what?"

"It was all my fault. I should have protected you. I was your mother, and it was my job."

Daniel picked up her hands. "None of this is your fault. It was dad's choice to leave the Amish and choose alcohol over his family. Over the last couple of days, I've come to realize I don't want to make the same mistakes."

"Oh, Daniel. Life is too short to hold onto so much anger. Nathan helped me learn that God knows each and every step in our journey. He puts people in front of us for a reason, and he challenges us to be more Christlike every day. There's no room to hold onto the past. We have a choice to change our tomorrows but never our yesterdays. I'll do whatever I can to help you move forward, but you have to stop looking back."

Daniel stood, grabbed the black felt hat off the back of the chair, and said, "Today's a new day and a new start for the both of us. I promise I'll go talk to Melvin, and you don't have to worry about me drinking; I've hurt too many people, and that is not who I want to be."

Holding his hand out, she stood and laid her hand in his and pulled him in for a hug and whispered. "God gives us grace; let's never forget that. I love you, son."

Daniel tucked her hand in the crook of his elbow and guided her to the door. "Now, let's go get you married off. Nathan's been barking orders at all of us for days. That man needs a good woman to calm him down, and I'm sure you're what he needs."

~~

Daniel sat at the back of the room and watched his mother in her new blue dress answer a series of marriage questions from the minister performing the ceremony.

He scanned the other side of the room and kept his eyes focused on Katie. She seemed to listen intently to the ceremony. With each question, Daniel studied Katie's reaction. While he certainly understood she was much too young to consider marriage, he couldn't help but think that someday they may be faced with the same questions. The minister's voice ehcoed off the walls as he directed each line to both Nathan and Marie.

Daniel had only attended one other Amish ceremony, and at the time, he didn't let it sink in as much as it was this time. He took each word to heart as he listened to each question.

Can you both confess that Gott has ordained marriage to be a union between one man and one wife, and do you also have the confidence that you are approaching marriage in accordance with the way you've been taught?

Both Nathan and Marie were quick to answer before the minister proceeded.

Do you also have the confidence, brother, that the Lord has provided this, our sister, as a marriage partner for you?

Unlike an English wedding where the bride and groom faced each other, both Nathan and Marie fixed their eyes on the minister in front of them. Nathan answered, and they continued.

Do you also promise your wife that if she should become in bodily weakness, sickness, or any circumstances need your help that you will care for her as fitting for a Christian husband?

Daniel could almost picture himself standing in Nathan's spot and would be quick to answer yes if Katie was standing beside him.

Do you promise together that you will come with love, forbearance, and patience, live with each other, and not part from each other until Gott will separate you in death?

Nathan answered yes, and Marie followed suit.

Daniel had grown up in the English world, but the simple ceremony with no exchange of rings or display of physical affection intrigued him. A God-centered simple marriage where two people joined as one to start a life guided by God, surrounded by their community.

When the ceremony ended, both Nathan and Marie moved to the corner *Eck* table, where they enjoyed a lunch prepared by their neighbors. Daniel didn't succumb to emotion, but the room was filled with a gentle calmness that moved him. Since both Nathan and Marie had been married before, there were no side sitters, or the normal routine of a typical wedding. With thoughts of his own father, he scanned the room, absent of Melvin.

Before heading to Jay, who stood at the back of the room talking to one of Nathan's stable boys, he stopped near Katie. She was filling water glasses at the benches that had been flipped over to tables. He leaned in close so only she could hear. "I'm sorry I had to cancel our Sugarcreek tour. I hope I can make it up to you."

Katie continued to move around the table while Daniel followed her on her heels.

"I wanted to take you sledding, but I'm afraid this bright sunshine might have melted off much of the snow from the best sledding hill in the area. Perhaps you'll let me treat you to supper?"

"Not today; Emma and I are trying to handle everything so Marie doesn't have to think about it. We even offered to keep an eye on Amos and Rachel this evening. Maybe tomorrow?"

"Five o'clock?"

Katie purposely brushed by him making contact with his side with her elbow. "I'll be ready," she whispered.

The jolt of electricity that moved up his arm forced a smile to his lips when she walked away. He shook his head to clear the effect she had on him and forced himself to walk toward Jay.

"Jay, I want to talk to your dad, but I don't see him."

Jay excused himself from the conversation he was having and nodded his head in the direction of the door, encouraging Daniel to follow him.

Once outside, Jay leaned back on the porch railing and said, "He wasn't feeling well today. We decided it best he stay home."

"Is he sick?"

Jay hesitated before answering. "What did you want to talk to him about?"

"I think it's time we get to the bottom of a few things."

Jay crossed his arms in front of his chest. "Have you given any more thought to the farm?"

"That's one of the things I want to talk to him about. While I understand the bind you're in, it's not what I have in mind for my future."

Jay didn't say a word as he stared motionlessly straight ahead. His eyebrows curled against each other, and his eyes widened. "Wasn't what I had in mind either, but sometimes your lot in life determines your path."

Daniel was quick to add. "I've come to the conclusion that no matter how hard I fight it, I'm a Shetler, but that name shouldn't dictate my future. The frustration I've had for your father is going away, and I do want to tell him that, but I also want to explain that this is his dream, not mine."

Jay shifted his weight to the other foot. "There is a chance I'll lose the farm if you don't come to help me. *Datt* has made it perfectly clear that the only way I can keep it is to convince you to stay."

Daniel walked to the edge of the step. "Well, then I guess we need to convince him that you can hire help that would be more willing to work a dairy farm than me. At some point, I'll need to go back to Willow Springs; my future is there."

Jay walked to where he stood and replied, "I believe he feels like giving you half of the farm will make up for turning his back on you."

"I need to set him straight. I don't need your farm as a peace offering. It's yours, not mine."

Jay walked down the steps but not before saying, "What he needs more than anything else is your forgiveness."

There was an urgency in Jay's voice that didn't sit quite right, and he followed his uncle to the barn. Their strides mimicked one another, and he asked, "What is it you're not saying?"

"He's dying."

Daniels boots sunk into the softening soil, and he reached out for Jay's arm. "What do you mean dying? Where'd this come from, and why didn't you tell me?"

"He didn't want you to know until he was certain you'd accept your rightful place in this family." Pulling his arm out of Daniel's grip, he said, "Do you think I'd follow you all over Willow Springs, saving your tail more than once if there wasn't something bigger going on here?"

Daniel's shoulders tensed. "More secrets. Why can't anyone be honest?"

"I don't like this any more than you do, but it's the man's last dying wish. Either you accept his apology and own up to being a Shetler, or you let the man go to his grave, agonizing over all the choices he made. It's up to you. Do what you want; I'm tired of babysitting you."

Raising his voice, "I already said I forgave him."

Jay went back to the barn, but not before saying, "Regardless of what you do, I have a dairy to run. Don't wait too long to talk to him. He doesn't have many days left."

Daniel headed in the opposite direction toward the horse stables yearning to find a few minutes alone to figure out what he really wanted. There was no doubt about it. He hoped to find a way to make it work with Katie, but to do that, he needed to return to Willow Springs and set things right with her father. He had a lot of making up to do if he expected him to accept him, and that would start with leaving his worldly ways aside to take rightful ownership alongside his ancestors. He wished his adoptive father could lend him the advice he needed, but he knew the answers he sought would only be found in Melvin Shetler.

Chapter 18
Willow Springs

Daniel agonized over the conversation he needed to have with his grandfather for two days. Along with Jay's insistence to not wait too long added to his unease. The early April sunshine warmed his face as he walked up the stairs to his grandparent's home, giving him a brief reprieve from his task.

Once Lillian answered the door, the sunken shadows below her eyes matched the heaviness that seeped outside. "We've been expecting you," she sighed.

He wiped his feet and followed her inside. Lillian moved toward the kitchen and pointed to the bench. "May I get you anything?"

"No, I'm good. How's Melvin?"

His grandmother twisted a lace hankie between her fingers. "Jay told you, didn't he?"

"He did."

Her upper lip quivered. "The doctor said there isn't anything else we can do but make him comfortable and keep him from getting too excited. He's been asking for you."

Daniel studied the closed bedroom door. "Is he awake?"

"When I left him a few minutes ago, he was sitting up reading the paper."

Daniel stood, and headed to the door.

"Daniel."

He stopped and followed his grandmother's voice. "Try not to upset him too much."

The soft, pleading tone of Lillian's words caught in the back of his throat as he swallowed hard in anticipation of the difficult conversation he was about to face. He took in a deep breath before he turned the knob and pushed the door open.

It had been weeks since he'd seen his grandfather, and the shell of the man was evident to his condition. The paper he held shook as he folded it and laid it aside and pointed to the chair near the window. "Closer," he mouthed in almost a whisper.

It didn't take Daniel but a second to understand his grandfather wanted him to move the chair next to the bed. He sat and rested his elbows on his knees while he waited for Melvin to get comfortable. When Daniel tried to assist him, he pushed his hand away and said, "Sit."

Melvin's voice wavered between a whisper and a throaty gurgle. "I've been expecting you."

Daniel sat up straight in his chair. "We have some things to talk about. To begin with, Jay's already told me what you expect of me."

"And?"

"I've spent the last couple of days rustling around with the answer I'd give you. Before we talk about that, let me tell you this; I've done some foolish things, and I suppose I owe a lot of thanks to Jay for saving me from most of it. I understand you put him up to watching over me. So, I guess some of that thanks goes to you as well."

His grandfather didn't say a word but kept his eyes looking over his wire-rimmed glasses, taking a labored breath with each rise of his chest.

Daniel tapped his thumbs on the arms of the rocking chair and let out a long breath before he continued. "I owe you an apology."

In a raspy voice, the old man said, "No."

"Regardless, the way I've treated you was uncalled for."

In slow motion, Melvin wiped his lips with the back of a bony knuckle before saying, "Forgiveness is as valuable to the one forgiving as it is to the one forgiven."

Daniel let his grandfather's words sink in before replying. "Someone told me once that forgiveness can be words or actions, and both mean the same. It was only until I remembered those words that I thought back to all you've done. It took me a while to see it, but I do recognize you spent your life looking out for me."

The heaviness Daniel carried around with him for the last nine months seemed to lighten in his presence. His grandfather pointed to the stand, and he responded by handing him a drink. After returning the glass to the table, he followed his shaking hand to the Bible. Struggling with turning the pages, he gave up and pushed it back to Daniel and said, "Ephesians 4:31."

Daniel shuffled through the thin pages until he found the verse. "Do you want me to read it?"

Melvin nodded his head and closed his eyes.

Daniel cleared his throat and began, *"Get rid of all bitterness, rage, anger, harsh words, and slander, as well as all type of evil behavior. Instead, be kind to each other, tenderhearted, forgiving one another, just as God through Christ has forgiven you."*

Melvin turned his head on the pillow and opened his eyes just as Daniel closed the book and let the words fill the void in the room. One single tear rolled from his grandfather's eye, and he muttered, "Please, forgive me."

The map of wrinkles on the old man's face softened when Daniel laid his palm across his withering hand. Lines were etched around his eyes that spoke of decades of responsibility, not only to his family, but his entire *g'may*. No words could describe how Daniel's heart melted as he watched the old man struggle to speak. There was an understanding in the quietness, and he said, "It's okay, we don't need to talk. Sleep if you need to.

"No, I must continue. Are we good?"

"Yes."

"What about the farm?"

Daniel clasped his hands before him and rested his elbow on the arm of the chair. "It's your dream, not mine."

"It's as much yours as it is Jay's."

"I understand that, but Jay can hire help. You don't have to give me half of this farm."

Melvin's disappointment showed in the way he fought to take a breath. "I owe that to you."

"No, you don't. You don't owe me a thing."

"What will you do, and where will you go?"

"Willow Springs is still my home, and I have some things to take care of there. If those things are settled, I may return, but working this farm is not what I'll be doing. Most likely, I'll be working for Nathan."

Melvin's voice cracked, "You're just like your father."

"I've been told that more than once, but I promise I'll only be looking to inspire his good qualities, not the ones that drove him from his home."

Melvin relaxed his head on the pillow, and within seconds, his eyes drifted close. Daniel continued to watch the man until his steady breathing turned into a light snore. He moved the chair back under the window and headed to the door. He took one last look at the man, who in so many ways had more to do with the man he'd become than his own father. Even if it took him this long to realize it.

His grandmother sat in a chair near the window with her head back, snoring softly. Maneuvering past her to the door, he eased it opened and left feeling more at ease than when he arrived. He sat on the top step, put his boots on, then headed to where Jay was working a team of horses in the pasture.

Jay set the brake on the manure spreader and hopped down from the bench seat. "How'd it go?"

"I think it went well. I did tell him I didn't need half of this farm."

"What will you do?"

"To start with, I'm going back to Willow Springs."

Jay extended his hand. "His offer will always stand. Regardless of what you do, this farm is as much mine as it is yours. It's his wish, and I'll always honor it."

Daniel squeezed his hand, "I appreciate it, and thank you for everything."

There was no doubt Jay knew what he was talking about, and they didn't need to muddle it up with more words. Jay nodded his head in the direction of his hat. "It suits you."

Daniel tipped the brim in Jay's direction. "I suppose it does."

~~

Emma knelt down and wrapped her arms around Rachel's shoulders. "I promise I'll come and visit again real soon. Summer will be here before you know it. You and Amos will be so busy playing outside you'll never notice I'm gone. Besides, who's going to help Marie learn about being Amish without your help?"

Rachel wiped the tear from her cheek on her shoulder and sniffled. "Who's going to take me sledding?"

Daniel laughed and picked her up while her satin ties twisted around her face when he swung her in a circle. "Winter is about over anyway, and you and Amos will find something else fun to do. I bet if you ask your *Datt*, he'll take you fishing. I saw some big bass swimming around in the pond just waiting to be caught."

Daniel set Rachel on her feet and patted Amos on the top of his head. "You're pretty good at hooking worms. How about you teach your *schwester* how to do it?"

Amos puffed out his chest. "I did good, didn't I?"

"You sure did, and by the time we come back, you'll be showing me a thing or two."

Marie reached out and took Amos and Rachel by the hand. "Come on, we need to let them get on their way, or they won't make it home before nightfall."

Emma took her turn giving everyone one last hug before climbing in next to Katie.

All three waved over their shoulder as Daniel pulled away from Bouteright Stables.

Katie reached up, turned the knob to the radio, held her finger to her lips, and looked at Emma. "Shhh, this is what it's all about, right?"

Daniel turned it down a notch and was quick to add. "I wouldn't get too used to that music; this is probably the last ride you'll have."

Emma looked around Katie. "You're serious, aren't you?"

"Things are about to change big time for your brother. If I expect Katie's dad to take me seriously, I'm going to need to earn his trust."

Emma let a few seconds fill the cab as she contemplated what Daniel would be dealing with. Becoming Amish was a big step, and even though she knew his heart was in the right place, she hoped he was putting his trust in *Gott* and not in the acceptance of Levi Yoder. She glanced at her best friend, it was no secret Katie was smitten with Daniel, and they had a language all of their own. Watching the two of them together left her longing for the way Samuel and she could have been. Her stomach did a little flip as she thought of seeing him again.

~~

Katie reached up and touched Daniel's arm. "You should leave me off at the end of the driveway."

Daniel flipped on the turn signal and slowed to almost a stop beside the Yoder's Strawberry sign. "No sense in prolonging the inevitable. I'm going to have to face your father at some point; it might as well be today."

Emma nodded toward the metal building. "Too late to back out now. There's Samuel and Levi."

Katie's posture stiffened as she took in a deep breath. Emma patted her knee. "Daniel's right. He might as well get it over with now."

"I can tell he is not happy. Please, let me off and go."

"Nope, not gonna happen. If your dad has a beef with me, the best way I can earn his respect starts right now."

Daniel pulled up beside Levi and opened his door. He tipped his straw hat and nodded. "Levi, Samuel."

Without extending a welcome, Levi walked to him. "Katie, this doesn't look like a bus. You were to let us know when to pick you up. Did you ride all the way from Sugarcreek with him?"

Katie walked up beside Daniel. "They were coming back to Willow Springs, and I saw no sense in paying for a bus ticket."

In a gruff voice, Levi stated, "I gave you explicit instructions about Daniel Miller. This is what I was afraid would happen. Going against your parent's wishes is just the start."

Katie's voice quivered, "I saw no harm in accepting a ride."

Talking as if Daniel was invisible, her father continued, "I'll have no daughter of mine being seen with the likes of Daniel Miller. That'll be the last time we'll have this conversation. Now go to the *haus* while I have a word with Daniel."

"But *Datt*."

"But *Datt* nothing, I told you to go to the *haus*!"

186

Katie peeked over her shoulder at Emma, who still sat in the truck. Emma nodded in her direction and mouthed, "Go, it's okay."

Emma's best friend's slumped shoulders walked across the yard. Out of the corner of her eye, she spotted Samuel. His glance was hardened and cold. Part of her wanted to go to him, but the thickness in the air prevented her from moving.

Daniel stood his ground and paused until Katie was out of earshot before he directed a comment in Levi's direction. "Mr. Yoder, I know you prefer I have nothing to do with Katie, but one of the reasons I came back to Willow Springs was to show you I can be trusted. My behavior the last few months was anything but respectable."

Daniel watched as Levi's jaw tightened, and he waited for a response.

"It's going to take more than a few words to change my mind, and it hasn't wavered. Stay away from my daughter. Have I made myself perfectly clear? Katie's not to set foot in that truck ever again, do you understand?"

Daniel felt the pressure on his shoulders and knew it would take more than one short conversation to convince Levi he wasn't a bad influence. Before he said anything he'd regret, he climbed back inside, but not before saying, "I can promise you she won't set foot back in this truck." He slammed the door and backed out of the driveway.

Emma remained quiet until he pulled out on Mystic Mill Road. "I'd say that was a pretty sneaky comment since you have plans on selling your truck."

"I didn't promise I wouldn't see her; I promised she wouldn't set foot back in this ole' girl. It's gonna take some work, but I was never one to shy away from a challenge."

Emma giggled and said, "For sure and certain."

It only took a few minutes before they pulled into her driveway. A sudden warmth filled Emma as she relished the idea of being home. Daniel pulled up in front of the barn. Matthew and her *datt* pushed the massive door aside and met them outside. As Daniel stepped out and extended his hand to Matthew, her *datt* came around the passenger door and engulfed her in a hug.

"Emma, you're home. For good or a visit?"

Emma laid her head on her *datt's* shoulder and whispered, "For good if you'll have me."

He patted her back in a tender embrace. She sensed her comment touched him in a way that left him struggling for words. She reached for her bag and followed him to the house. Turning only once in Daniel's direction, he waved her on and turned his attention back to Matthew.

Chapter 19

Sorry

"What's up with the hat and suspenders?" Matthew asked.

"It's time for a change."

"You don't say. What's Katie think about that?"

"She hasn't said much, but I'm not too certain she thinks I can do it."

"I have to admit, I've yet met a man that could give up everything the English world has to offer. If you're serious, you'll be the first around here."

"I'm certain it's going to be challenging, but if I can convince the bishop to give me a chance, that's half the battle. I promised my mother I wouldn't follow in the same steps as my father, and even though I let his world take hold of me, I want to live right by my birth name. I've already talked to my adoptive parents, and they're very understanding in me wanting to accept my Amish roots."

Matthew furled his eyebrows together. "This wouldn't have anything to do with Katie, would it?"

"I'm not gonna lie that she doesn't have something to do with it, but my decision is solely my own."

"It won't be easy; you'll have to learn the language, and you'll need to become baptized. As much ruckus as you raised in this town, I would assume the bishop and the ministers are going to be pretty hard on you."

"Oh, believe me, I've already heard the wrath of Levi Yoder. I figure if I can earn his respect back, the rest will come easy."

Matthew rested his foot on the truck bumper. "I'm certain the best way to Levi Yoder's good side is to stay away from Katie. By the look on your face, that will be your biggest obstacle. Levi's made it clear he wants nothing to do with you or your wild ways. My advice, if you care to take it, is to keep Katie out of the picture. She still lives under his roof and will be expected to follow his rules. If you come between him and his daughter, you'll end up with the short end of the stick."

Daniel turned and propped his foot on the tire. "I suppose you're right but keeping Katie out of the picture won't be easy, but if that's what I need to do, so be it."

Matthew headed to the barn and motioned Daniel to follow him. "I received a letter from Nathan a few weeks ago extending his offer for me to help him board horses from the stable. I've been busy getting the barn ready, come see what I've done."

"Yeah, he did say something about that. He's hoping you'll spend some time at the stables first."

"I told him as soon as the weather breaks, I'll be over. My *datt* hasn't been doing so good the last few months, but now that Emma's home, maybe that will help, and I can take off for a few weeks."

Daniel caught up to his long strides. "Now that I'm back in Willow Springs, and if you're up for it, perhaps I could teach you what you need to know to board Nathan's horses. I assume he didn't realize I was heading back here for good."

Matthew stopped in his tracks. "If you're serious about staying around, perhaps we could run this boardinghouse together?"

"I hadn't given a thought to what I was going to do once I got back here. I burned all my bridges at the Feed and Seed. I knew I'd have to find a job. But maybe helping you is the answer. I'm certain Nathan won't have a problem with it."

Matthew slapped Daniel on the back and headed to the back of the barn. "I need to get this settled before fall."

"Does that have anything to do with the celery seed Katie caught Rebecca and Anna buying?"

The corner of Matthews lipped turned upward. "Let's say a certain young woman wouldn't take too kindly to her new husband not having a job to support her."

"Well, it's about time, even though I don't understand what Sarah Mast sees in you."

"I could say the same about you. For what it's worth, I'd say the both of us are pretty lucky."

~~

Emma followed her father through the side door and set her bag down in time for Anna to screech. "Emma, you're home!"

Emma glanced over Anna's shoulder in time for Rebecca to spit out a welcome. "So, the prodigal daughter returns again. How long this time?"

In one swift move, Emma's *datt* grabbed the back of Rebecca's arm and squeezed. "I'll not have this again! Emma is as much a part of this family as you are, and I will not have you chase her away again. You either drop the attitude, or you will be the one leaving."

Rebecca pulled her arm from his grip, "Ouch!"

"I mean it, daughter, I'll tolerate this no more. Right here and right now, get off your chest, whatever it is bothering you, or you'll be paying the bishop a visit. I'll not have strife in this *haus*."

191

Rebecca rubbed her arm. "Fine, I'll tell you what my issue is. She comes and goes in and out of this family like she has no responsibilities. You worship the ground she walks on like *Mamm* did. If she wouldn't have caused her so much grief, she might still be with us."

Emma bit her bottom lip. She knew Rebecca blamed her, but what she didn't realize was the pain she'd have to witness in her *schwesters* eyes. It took all the courage she had to walk over and open her arms to her.

"I miss her as much as you do, and if you need to blame someone, blame me, but don't let your hurt and anger spill out to this family. I'm your *schwester* and will always be. You, *Datt*, Anna, and Matthew are my family. This is my home. Please, Rebecca, stop. We all miss her, and this *haus*, this home, and this family will never be the same, but we have to settle this for her sake."

She paused a few seconds before continuing. "Forgiveness has been embedded in our souls since we were *kinner,* and there's no room for anger. It only pushes *Gott* aside. If any of us will get through this, we must do everything to rely on and trust *Gott's* plan. It was her time. We couldn't change that no matter how hard we tried. It was not our place to change her story. It was written, her chapter complete, and her book closed. But her legacy lives on in this family. Rebecca, I understand you're angry with me, but no good is coming of this; you're only pushing *Gott* out of your heart, and *Mamm* wouldn't like that."

When Rebecca didn't respond to her open arms, she dropped her hands and sat motionless in a chair at the table. They all waited for Rebecca to say something ...anything. When she refused to move from her stance beside the counter, Emma lowered her head on folded arms and begged. "Please, *Gott,* tell me what to do; I've tried everything."

Within a few seconds, Rebecca's hand met her shoulder and Anna stepped beside them. Anna leaned over and rested her cheek on the top of Emma's starched white *kapp*, and within seconds the three *schwesters* mourned together.

Chapter 20
I'll wait forever...

T he sun had started to descend, and its late afternoon rays spilled through Katie's bedroom window and landed on her cheek. Their warmth began to dry the moisture on her pillow. For the past two hours, she pleaded with her parents to give Daniel another chance. Her *datt* was relentless in his stand, and her heart ached as she planned how she could see him. If only she would have remembered to ask Emma for her phone.

Sitting up and wiping her cheeks with the back of her hand, she grabbed a blue scarf, tied it around her chin, and headed downstairs. She stopped at the front door long enough to wrap a shawl around her shoulders and took a minute to leave a note letting them know she'd gone to Emma's.

The roar of Daniel's engine over the ridge alerted her attention and forced her to pray her *datt* wouldn't hear. Daniel stopped beside her and rolled down his window.

"You've been crying?"

She wiped to stray tear from her cheekbone. "It's nothing I can't work out."

"Does this have anything to do with me?"

"We can't talk here. Can we go for a ride?"

"Are you sure you want to do that? That will aggravate him even more, and I don't want you to disobey him."

"I'm sure it will, but at this point, I'm so mad I don't even care."

She didn't even give him a chance to respond before she walked around the front of the truck and hopped inside. "What he fails to remember is I am on my *Rumspringa,* and I have every right to push the limits if I so choose."

Once she was inside, he drove past her driveway and headed into town. "So, where do you want to go?"

"Not to town! Someone will see me for sure. How about we go to the covered bridge?"

An array of emotions twirled around in Katie's stomach. One of excitement to be so close to Daniel and the other an edge of defiance that she didn't quite understand. Her whole life, she did what her parents expected of her. Still, her ever-growing fondness for Daniel gave her the confidence to step out of her boundaries.

When they were safely away, Daniel motioned her to move closer. Once she settled into the middle of the bench seat, he laid his hand on her knee and squeezed. Without hesitation, she laid her hand over his and rubbed the back of his knuckles.

In not much more than a whisper, she said, "I'm not so sure my *datt* will ever come around. Even if you do become Amish, he thinks you're too much older than me. He wants me to find a boy my own age. I'm afraid he'll never accept you."

He patted her knee, "Now you leave your dad to me. I'm serious about courting you properly; he'll see my intentions are pure. Right now, all he sees or what he remembers is what he's heard around town. I have every intention of proving to him and this community, I can be trusted. About me being so much older, it's just a number. I'll wait as long as it takes, and if that means waiting until your eighteen, so be it."

He pulled off to the side of the road right before the covered bridge and turned in his seat to face her. "Look at me, we have lots of time to work on your dad. I'm not going anywhere, and I'm in for the long haul. I realize you're only sixteen, and if you were my daughter, I'd probably be doing the same thing. We are in no hurry."

He reached up and laid his finger below her chin and kissed the tip of her nose. "Now, where's that smile that captured my heart?"

Katie lifted her eyes until they met his. "What if you get tired of waiting?"

He placed his hand on the back of her head and pulled her so close she could feel his breath on her lips. "I'll never tire of waiting for this." The moisture on his lips mixed with hers as a tiny sigh gurgled in her throat.

~~

It had been two weeks since Emma had returned to Willow Springs. Even though things with Rebecca had taken a turn for the better, she still hadn't gotten up enough nerve to confront Samuel. That morning, she'd overheard Edna Graber speak of Samuel at The Mercantile. While she was sure she only mentioned his name when she saw her walk in the door; she couldn't help but feel a twinge of apprehension in confronting him. There was no doubt Edna felt threatened by her return.

The bright spring sun warmed her face as she raked winter's leftover leaves out of the garden. It was still too early to plant, but an unexpected warm spell had left her yearning to be outside. The clip-clop of an approaching buggy turned her attention toward the driveway. She expected it to stop at the furniture shop, but it pulled alongside the fence instead. The heavy yellow canvas had been rolled up, allowing her to accept Samuel's warm greeting.

"You're itching to get your hands in that soil, aren't you?"

"You know me well. It might be only April, but I already have my seeds bought and the garden all planned out. Before long, the crocuses and daffodils will be blooming, and I'll be planting spinach and spring onions."

Samuel didn't say a word but continued to look her way. When the silence between them became uncomfortable, she asked, "What brings you here?"

He hesitated only for a moment. "You."

"Me?"

"Yes, you. Is that so strange?"

"No, I guess not. But I think Edna would think otherwise."

"Edna? What does she have to do with me stopping to see you?"

"A lot since word has it that you're courting her."

Adjusting his tone, he said, "Courting her, who told you that?"

"I guess I assumed, and I pretty much told you, you were free to do so."

"What you told me and what you assume is wrong. When you left, yes, I was mad. I needed time to adjust the plans in my own head."

He set the break and hopped down from his seat and walked to where she stood. Resting one foot on the edge of the fence rail, he leaned in closer on both elbows. "I'm just gonna spit out what I came here to say."

She tucked a piece of loose hair back under her blue scarf and waited for him to continue.

"You had a lot on your plate, and I had no right to rush you into something you weren't ready for. I think I did more harm than good by telling you what I had planned. I've done a lot of soul-searching these last couple of months and no matter how I play it in my head, the final outcome always involves you."

"No, I was the one not being fair."

Samuel held up his hand. "Now wait, let me finish before I lose my nerve. I rushed you, and I pushed you away. I guess what I came here to tell you was; I'll wait for you no matter how long."

Emma released her hand from the rake and took one step closer, resting her hand on his. "Do you think you can wait until I'm eighteen? That's only a little more than a year?"

"As I said, I'll wait forever."

He covered her hand with his other and leaned in until their foreheads touched. With no thought of her family seeing them, he added, "What's a few more months if I get you for the rest of our lives?"

Epilogue

L ate October was a time for celebration as the Apple Blossom Inn held its annual Harvest Festival. The simmering pots of apple butter combined with art and craft vendors filled the grounds around the inn. Emma was happy they took a break from helping Sarah get her family's farm ready for the wedding reception.

Emma turned to face her *schwesters* and nodded to the snack table. "I'll catch up with you later; I'm going to go help myself to some apple cider and doughnuts."

Anna snickered. "You don't fool us; all you want to do is get closer to Samuel. You couldn't be more obvious if it was written all over your face."

Emma ignored her comment and let the magnetic pull Samuel had on her guide her way.

Samuel had one leg propped up on an overturned bucket with both forearms resting on his knee. His straw hat askew on his head added to his boyish charm. Emma smiled to herself as she enjoyed the view from afar. During the past six months, they'd spent every other Sunday night planning for their future. Engrossed in a conversation with Daniel, Samuel didn't see her approach. It was Daniel who acknowledged her presence.

"Katie said she wasn't sure you'd make it since you've been over to Sarah's."

"Sarah insisted we come to the festival, and I'm glad she did. We have about everything ready, and it can't get here quick enough for as antsy as Matthew is." Daniel and Samuel both laughed, but it was Samuel who added, "I'd suppose I'd be the same way."

Emma caught the warm way he looked at her, raising one eyebrow insinuating how he'd be on his own wedding day. A little dance was going on inside with the thought of perhaps next year, at this time, she'd be planning her own special day.

Daniel waved his hand over her head, trying to catch Katie's attention. "Katie, over here."

Emma turned in the direction of Daniel's gaze; her best friend smiled to match the light in her *bruders* eyes. There was no mistake the summer did for Daniel and Katie the same as it did for her and Samuel. The four of them, appointed to be side sitters at Matthew and Sarah's wedding, had a common goal. They had become inseparable all summer as they enjoyed countless picnics, fishing excursions, and plenty of rides to the Dairy Bar. It bloomed their friendship into something that would last a lifetime.

Katie stopped at Emma's side. "I've been looking all over for you. I saw Anna and Rebecca, and they pointed me in this direction." She leaned in and whispered in Emma's ear, "I should've known if I found my *bruder,* I'd find you."

Emma squeezed her friend's arm ever so lightly."Shhhh..."

Katie's lip turned upward. "It's just the four of us; it's no secret, as it's no secret about Daniel and me. Even my *datt* warmed up to the idea now that Daniel is taking baptismal classes and sold his truck."

Daniel repositioned the straw hat on his head and hooked his fingers under his suspenders. "I'm not saying it wasn't easy to break through Levi Yoder, but after a few man-to-man conversations, he knew I wasn't going to back down, and he gave up."

In one swift move, Samuel kicked the bucket and turned it right side up, and added, "To be quite honest, I think *mamm* had more to do with it than your man to man. Katie and I heard her reminding him how much her own *datt* would have picked anyone but him to marry his daughter."

Katie moved closer to Daniel's side. "I've thanked her more than once. I think he's turning a blind eye and coming to terms with me seeing you." Daniel wrapped his arm around her shoulder and pulled her close for a side hug.

Emma tilted her head and smiled as she listened to the three people's conversation that meant the most to her. A *bruder* she didn't know she had, a best friend soon to be sister-in-law, and the love of her life. *Gott* had blessed her in more ways than one. He proved to her repeatedly if she put her trust in Him, he would always provide. In the sixteen years her *mamm* had raised her, the one thing that stood out more substantial than anything else was that she believed *Gott* had a plan. *Mamm* often said it wasn't her place to question His plan, just trust He always knew what was best.

Emma was certain she would strive to live the same way her Amish *mamm* had for the rest of her life. To live every day to the fullest, not regretting yesterday's or agonizing over the tomorrow's but finding joy in today.

Isaiah 43:18-19: (NLV) "Do not remember the things that have happened before. Do not think about the things of the past. See, I will do a new something. It will begin happening now. Will you not know about it? I will even make a road in the wilderness, and rivers in the desert.

Read more of Emma's story in the
first book of the:
The Amish Women of Lawrence County Series - Emma - Book 1
https://tracyfredrychowski.com/emma/

Emma

The Amish Women of Lawrence County - Book 1

E mma snuggled in close to Samuel and rested her hand on his arm. She took in the slow rise of his chest and thanked *Gott* for all the blessings he provided them over the past year. The winter wind whistled around the small *doddi haus* they called home while their new one was being built in the field next to his parents. Samuel and her *bruder* Daniel were putting in long hours, but the progress was slow with no heat and short days.

In the wee hours right before dawn, Emma treasured the few moments of her husband's warmth before the alarm jolted him from slumber. As she lifted her knee and laid it across his thigh, a small jolt from her protruding tummy woke him.

In a raspy voice he said, "I swear that boy will come out running."

She moved her cheek to his chest, "What makes you so sure it's a boy?"

He moved a wisp of her honey blonde hair from his chin and kissed the top of her head. "Wishful thinking, I guess."

Emma knew his heart was set on a baby boy, and she hoped and prayed if it was a girl, he'd love her the same.

Samuel turned on his side until their noses touched. He kissed the center of her forehead and squeezed her tight. "You've made me the happiest man." He patted her stomach. "This *bobbi* is just one of many I want to fill our home."

She lifted her head and kissed his chin. "I hope you still say that when the cries and the diapers pile up."

A nervous giggle etched deep in his throat. "Cries, no problem. Diapers? I might need to go to the barn if too many of them pile up."

Emma lifted her hand and pushed his chest, making him fall to his back. "Oh no, we're in this together! Cries and diapers and teething and colic and bad behavior ...the whole gamut. If I don't get to pick and choose, neither do you!"

She rolled off the bed, grabbed her robe to cover her white cotton nightdress and he engulfed her in a hug from behind. He nuzzled her neck, patted her bottom, and said, "I'll start the coffee."

Emma reached for the hairbrush, sat down on the bed, and undid the long braid that fell over her shoulder. With each stroke she made through her waist-length hair, she said a prayer of thanksgiving. Her life, as she saw it, was perfect. She had the man of her dreams, a new *haus*, her best friend and sister-in-law Katie Miller lived across the street, and she was seven months pregnant with their first child. In her eyes, *Gott* had truly blessed her. With her hair still down, she pulled her robe closed and headed to the kitchen. The white porcelain pot on the stove was already starting to gurgle as Samuel set two cups out on the table.

She filled a tiny pitcher with cream and sat it near his place at the head of the table. "What are your plans today?"

"Daniel and I are going to get back at the *haus*. He has been a big help, and if we keep at it, by the time the baby comes, we'll be able to move in. But first, we have to go over and pick up the kitchen cupboards from your *datt's* shop. If all goes well, we'll get those hung today."

Emma pulled both hands up to her chin and clapped, as a smile encased her face.

"I guess by that little happy dance, you're excited."

"Now, don't get me wrong, I love living here, but to have my own kitchen, and one you built for me, for sure and certain, it's a woman's dream."

"All I care is you keep that smile on your face and I'll hang cupboards every day."

She poured the hot brown liquid into his cup and set the kettle on a trivet in the middle of the table. He pulled her into his lap. "How about I stay home today?"

"Oh no, you don't!" She pushed herself back up.

"I have work to do, and so do you. Katie's coming over, and we're working on a new baby quilt, and I want to make some gingersnaps before she gets here. Let me get you breakfast so you can get out of here, and I can get to work."

"I see how it goes. Katie comes, and I'm out the door!"

She slapped him with the towel. "Don't be silly. No one is more important than you."

~~

Samuel whistled as he pulled on his boots and secured the black felt hat to his head. He winked at his *fraa* and closed the door behind him. An early winter storm covered the steps and sidewalk with six inches of fresh snow. He skimmed the porch for the snow shovel and remembered he'd left it on the back stoop, deciding he'd shovel it later. His long strides headed to the barn and he tipped his head to block the wind as he ducked inside the metal building. Amongst the implements they used for strawberry season; his new family buggy sat just inside the door. He effortlessly lifted a shaft in each hand and backed the buggy out the double doors. Before he had a chance to walk to the horse barn, Emma called his name from the front door.

She held up a thermos. "Samuel, your coffee."

Before he had a chance to holler back, *the steps were slippery*, he saw a flash of white as her nightclothes and wheat-colored hair spilled to the ground.

"Emma... nooooo!"

As if in slow motion, he ran to the crumpled form laying at the bottom of the steps. He knelt beside her, placed his hand under the back of her head, and warmth penetrated his glove. His bellowing scream pierced the frozen air. "Heeeelp!"

Read more of Emma's story.

https://tracyfredrychowski.com/emma/

What did you think?

Irst of all, thank you for purchasing Secrets of Willow Springs - Book 3. I hope you enjoyed all three books in this series.

You could have picked any number of books to read, but you picked this book, and for that, I am incredibly grateful. I hope it added value and quality to your everyday life. If so, it would be nice if you could share this book with your friends and family on Social Media.

If you enjoyed this book and found some benefit in reading it, I'd like to hear from you and hope that you could take some time to post a review on Amazon. Your feedback and support will help me improve my writing craft for future projects.

If you loved visiting Willow Springs, I invite you to sign up for my private email list where you'll get to explore more of the characters of this Old-Order Amish Community.

Sign up here>> https://dl.bookfunnel.com/v9wmnj7kve and download the novella that starts the series *The Amish Women of Lawrence County*.

Glossary of "Deutsch" Words

Ausbund. Amish songbook.

bruder. Brother

datt. Father or dad.

doddi. Grandfather.

doddi haus. A small house next to main house.

fraa. Wife.

g'may. Community.

haus. House.

ja. "Yes."

kapp. Covering or prayer cap.

kinner. Children.

mamm. Mother or mom.

mei lieb. "My love."

mommi. Grandmother.

Ordnung. Order or set of rules the Amish follow.

rumspringa. "Running around" period.

schwester. Sister.

singeon. Singing/youth gathering.

The Amish are a religious group typically referred to as Pennsylvania Dutch, Pennsylvania Germans, or Pennsylvania Deutsch. They are descendants of early German immigrants to Pennsylvania, and their beliefs center around living a conservative lifestyle. They arrived between the late 1600s and the early 1800s to escape religious persecutions in Europe. They first settled in Pennsylvania with the promise of religious freedom by William Penn. Most Pennsylvania Dutch still speak a variation of their original German language as well as English.

About the Author

Tracy Fredrychowski lives a life similar to the stories she writes. Striving to simplify her life, she often shares her simple living tips and ideas on her website and blog at tracyfredrychowski.com.

Growing up in rural northwestern Pennsylvania, country living was instilled in her from an early age. As a young woman, she was traumatized by the murder of a young Amish woman in her rural Pennsylvania community. She became dedicated to sharing stories of their simple existence. She inspires her readers to live God-centered lives through faith, family, and community. If you would like to enjoy more of the Amish of Lawrence County, she invites you to join her on

209

Facebook. There she shares her friend Jim Fisher's Amish photography, recipes, short stories, and an inside look at her favorite Amish community nestled in northwestern Pennsylvania, deep in Amish Country.

Made in the USA
Monee, IL
11 October 2021

79819774R10132